DANGEROUS WATERS

DANGEROUS WATERS

An ADVENTURE on TITANIC

GREGORY MONE

ROARING BROOK PRESS

NEW YORK

Photo credits: pg. 223, Harvard University Archives, HUD 307.04.5; pg. 224 & 225, HEW 12.12. 25, Harry Elkins Widener Collection, Harvard University; pg. 228 bottom, courtesy of the Library of Congress, Prints and Photographs Division, George Grantham Bain Collection; pg. 229 top, © Underwood & Underwood/Corbis; pg. 229 bottom, photo courtesy of the Library of Congress, Prints and Photographs Division.

Library of Congress Cataloging-in-Publication Data
Mone, Gregory.
  Dangerous waters : an adventure on Titanic / Gregory Mone. — 1st ed.
    p. cm.
  Summary: Determined to focus on work rather than books, as his father had, twelve-year-old Patrick Waters leaves Belfast as a steward on the Titanic, but the very wealthy Harry Widener arranges to tutor him, drawing Patrick into association with thieves seeking Harry's very rare edition of Francis Bacon's Essays.
  ISBN 978-1-59643-673-2
  [1. Conduct of life—Fiction. 2. Books and reading—Fiction. 3. Widener, Harry Elkins, 1885–1912—Fiction. 4. Robbers and outlaws—Fiction.
5. Tutors and tutoring—Fiction. 6. Social classes—Fiction. 7. Titanic (Steamship)—Fiction.] I. Title.
  PZ7.M742Dan 2012
  [Fic]—dc23

                                                          2011018652

Roaring Brook Press books are available for special promotions and premiums.
For details contact: Director of Special Markets, Holtzbrinck Publishers.

First edition 2012
Printed in the United States of America by
RR Donnelley & Sons Company, Harrisonburg, Virginia

3   5   7   9   10   8   6   4   2

To Dylan

CONTENTS

SAVED BY CERVANTES

Long after midnight, a short-haired man of average height crossed from London's Kensington Gardens to Mount Street, headed east. Mr. John Francis Berryman had walked silently through the damp, thick grass of the park, but now his over-sized heels clacked loudly as he stepped onto the cobblestone street. The noise was unacceptable, even if no other souls were out at that hour. He would have to be more careful. Silent. Ideally he would proceed unnoticed, steal the book, and return to his small flat within the hour.

Steal: such a harsh, stubborn word. Was this truly stealing? He planned to return the book once he and Mr. Rockwell found what they needed. And besides, the book's owner, Harry Elkins Widener, was so wealthy that he could hardly be stolen from. They had been in school together, at Harvard College, and Harry never once had to worry about money. His family owned streetcar lines, railroads, and office buildings. He lived in a one-hundred-five-room mansion and had begun amassing his noted collection of rare—and, in Berryman's estimation, largely superficial—books at a mere twenty-one years of age.

Berryman, on the other hand, dragged behind him a heavy chain of debts. He owed money to his grocer, his tailor, numerous professors and colleagues, even one of his students. His shoe-maker was holding no less than three pairs of his boots, vowing not to restore them until he was paid in full, and the local baker refused to loan him so much as a roll.

None of this was Mr. Berryman's fault. The cruel, unbalanced world had thrust him into his present predicament. And this, he believed, granted him the right to *borrow* from those more fortunate. He walked carefully ahead.

South Audley Street was all shadows. No lights shone through the windows looking over the narrow street. No candles burned, no streetlamps glowed, and Quaritch Booksellers, he noted with pleasure, was particularly lifeless.

A low scuffling sound startled him. He turned, grabbed his knife, saw nothing; a rat, presumably.

At the door to the shop he glanced once more along the length of the dark, wet street, inserted the key he'd lifted off that foolish clerk earlier in the day, and entered. He took a moment to bask: He might not have been the best of thieves, but he doubted that any other scholars possessed such skill.

Inside, he breathed in the musty, aged smell of thousands of books. That book dust was fresh sea air to him. So much weathered leather, so many brittle yellowing pages. All that hardened cloth and browned book-binding glue. He found it completely invigorating.

Yet he had no time to browse the shelves. He had an assignment. He was to procure the rare second edition of Sir Francis Bacon's *Essaies* before Quaritch shipped it off to Widener's Philadelphia mansion.

The door to the old book dealer's second floor office was open. The electric lights would be too bright, too conspicuous, so he lit a small candle with the deft flick of a match and examined several boxes of books stacked about the room. Widener's supply was sitting near the door, packaged and ready to sail for America.

The anticipation forced his hands to quiver, but the value of the books demanded that he work with the utmost care. He delicately cut open the box and removed each precious volume. The books were either preserved in hard clothbound cases or wrapped in several layers of soft felt.

The size and thickness of each item varied, but the book he sought would be thin. The *Essaies* were really little more than an extended pamphlet, so there was no need to inspect the larger volumes. This realization allowed him to arrive sooner at a terribly unfortunate conclusion.

The *Essaies* were gone.

But how? Berryman knew that Widener had instructed Quaritch to buy the book for him. Quaritch had completed the sale a few days before. All of Widener's other purchases were there. The old bookseller had to have the *Essaies*.

He rushed to Quaritch's desk, sat in the old man's place, laid his hands on the leather-topped surface. Applying more care than the dealer deserved, Berryman opened Quaritch's ledger and flipped through the thin, dry pages. His hands and fingers were shaking. His jaw locked shut. On the last page he found it: A note from that very day recording a visit from Harry Elkins Widener. Mr. Berryman held his candle close and read:

> *Visit from HEW. Nice young man. Paid in full and looked upon the books with angelic devotion. Should be a lucrative customer. Interested in Cruikshank and RLS in particular. Very, very happy to see that the Bacon was his. Ordered the lot to be sent to Philadelphia, except for the Essaies, which he's taking aboard the new ocean liner, Titanic. If I'm shipwrecked, he said, the Bacon will go with me.*

The spoiled, rich fool! Berryman slapped his hand down hard on the desk.

A moment later he heard footsteps. Someone was ascending the stairs: The glow of a candle on the wall outside the door brightened with each step.

Berryman moistened the pads of his forefinger and thumb with his tongue, prepared to extinguish his own candle, then stopped himself. The person would have seen the glow. If he were to extinguish the flame now, they'd know for sure that there was an intruder and call for help. Instead Berryman rushed to the door and waited, standing aside.

The careful footsteps stopped outside the office, and then an old, hunched-over figure walked through. Berryman could assume no risk: He leaped forward and pushed the man to the floor, but the man grasped Berryman's ankle as he fell. Berryman tumbled as he tried to flee.

The candle still glowed; in the dim light he could see that it was old Quaritch himself.

Berryman tried to shake and kick his way free, but the old bookseller would not let go.

"Thief!" Quaritch yelled. "Help, thief!"

Berryman promptly struck the old man on the head with the heel of his boot. Quaritch released him, whimpering like a pitiful, injured dog. There was little choice now, as the bookseller had surely seen him. Berryman reached inside his coat and removed the knife.

The shouts for help ceased. Quaritch stared at the blade, confused and frightened at once. Berryman always thought that his preferred weapon, a knife typically used to slice free the uncut pages of newly printed books, was uniquely clever, and he was happy to see that the irony was not lost on Quaritch.

The old man crawled away backwards, his knees upturned like a spider's legs. A rivulet of blood ran down his forehead, spreading in the wrinkles of his brow.

Quaritch stopped at the base of one of the room's many mountainous bookshelves and began pulling books down from the shelves, surrounding himself with the texts as if he were trying to form an impenetrable, book-built shield. He piled them on his lap, in front of his stomach, and clutched them to his chest.

In the dim candlelight Berryman saw clearly that they were rare, valuable classics. *Little Dorrit* by Charles Dickens, Herman Melville's *Moby Dick*, even a copy of one of Mr. Berryman's favorites, Cervantes' *Don Quixote*.

He had no choice but to lower the knife; he could not bear the thought of such precious books stained with that old man's blood. Most of all, he could not hurt the *Quijote*. He pocketed his weapon and moved toward the door, deeper into the shadows. "You have not seen me," he said. "I have stolen nothing."

"Yes, yes," Mr. Quaritch answered, "I have not seen you."

Mr. Berryman hurried down the stairs, out to South Audley Street, and back toward the park.

"Thief! Thief!" he heard the old, frightened bookseller shouting weakly in the distance.

But he was not a thief. John Francis Berryman was a scholar. A man of the mind and a lover of books.

PRIDE OF BELFAST

In the kitchen of O'Neill's, a small alehouse crammed between a funeral parlor and a shoemaker's shop in the heart of Belfast, young Patrick Waters plunged the last of a night's worth of glasses into the sink. He dunked it beneath the soapy surface, wiped it once with a rag, rinsed it quickly, and set it to dry on a white towel spread across the counter. Then he stopped, attempted to dry his water-wrinkled hands on his partially-soaked shirt, and listened.

Patrick, twelve years old and tall, was a very good listener. He could hear whispered words at a great distance, and although there was no scientific reason to suggest this was true, most people who knew him attributed this ability to his embarrassingly large ears. They were big enough for a man twice his size and leaned out, and slightly forward, at the tops, as if they were designed to catch sounds.

He let his hair grow long enough to cover his ears, yet they still poked out far enough to earn him a handful of undesirable nicknames. Boys at his old school, St. Mark's, called him Jack the Donkey, and the men at O'Neill's referred to him as Pegasus, the famous winged horse. "Fly off with those gargantuan ears and fetch me another stout, Pegasus!" they'd shout laughing.

Now, with his work for the day finished, Patrick aimed those ears out toward the bar, on the other side of the swinging door leading in and out of the kitchen. The place was nearly empty. Only Mr. Joyce, the barman, and a few customers remained, and they were talking, as they often had in recent weeks, about *Titanic*, the great ocean liner that was being built right there in Belfast.

The voices were familiar: the bearlike growl of Mr. McNulty, who owned a small bookstore on Donegall Street; the thick country accent of Mr. Reilly, and, of course, Mr. Joyce's deep, assured baritone.

"She's finished!" Mr. Reilly declared. "Every last rivet is secure."

"John McKeown tells me there's still painting to be done," Mr. Joyce put in. He always had some scrap of rare information at hand.

"You would save that for last, though, wouldn't you?" Mr. McNulty growled. "Like any lady, *Titanic* will wait until the last minute to apply her makeup."

As the men laughed, Patrick tucked in his soap-splattered shirt, grabbed his wool coat and cap, and hurried out of the kitchen. Mr. Joyce, bald and red-faced, with a pencil behind each ear, rested his thick forearms on the dark, square bar. The men sat leaning on the bar before him, each of them halfway through their stouts.

"We are all washed up, Mr. Joyce," Patrick said. "Will I be going home now?"

His boss nodded, granting him permission to leave.

"Is it true your brother has a position on the ship?" Mr. Reilly asked.

"I wouldn't know," Patrick answered. "He's been at sea. I haven't heard from him for months."

"I would guess he'll be on that ship. I'd expect nothing less from the lad," Mr. Joyce said. "Your brother knows well what I've told you many times before, Patrick. You must associate yourself with greatness in this life."

Mr. Reilly looked around the pub, then placed his large hands on the bar. "Is this greatness then?" he asked with a laugh.

A bar towel flew his way, but then Mr. Joyce smiled.

Mr. McNulty raised a glass and tilted it toward Patrick. "Be sure to tell your mother that we've nearly sold the last of your father's books. And in only six months! Ah, the collection that man had," he said, turning to Mr. Joyce. "The greatest adventures and stories. Stevenson, Kipling, plus the Romans. He was a learned man, John Waters, a true scholar of the street. Though, of course, you wouldn't know it if you saw him after he'd downed his first few pints of—"

"Thank you, Mr. McNulty," Patrick interrupted. "I'll be sure to let her know."

The Waters' home was two stories tall, narrow, lonely, and usually quiet, but as Patrick approached that night he could hear laughter from the street. The front windows, at least one of them cracked, were sweating. There had to be several people inside; he thought he heard his brother.

Patrick burst in smiling and was thrown to the floor within seconds.

"Bigger every day but no faster!" James said.

Sitting on Patrick's chest, with his knees on his younger brother's shoulders, James threw several pretend punches. Patrick was destined to be tall and thin, like their father, but James was built like the Kelly men on his mother's side. If the Waters men were trees, the Kellys were boulders. Patrick squirmed, but there was no way he'd break free.

One of his brother's friends sat at the rough hewn wooden table, next to his mother. James began to cough—the familiar dry, grating cough of a man who worked with coal. Patrick twisted to one side and pushed him away, while James punched himself in the chest to quiet the rumbling.

"The cough of a working man!" his mother declared.

The other young man raised his glass. "Precisely, Mrs. Waters! The song of a stout-hearted coal man."

James settled his breathing and lunged at Patrick, then stopped, smiled, and embraced him. This was his brother: big-hearted and quick-tempered, as likely to hug as to hit you.

They were almost the same height now, Patrick noticed. He was eight years younger than James, but he'd be taller in a matter of months.

"Sit with us," James said, pulling out a chair. "This is Martin Blaney, of King Street, a man with fireproof skin. I've seen him palm a hunk of hot coal that would've seared the hands of a lesser man. All four of his brothers are trimmers, too, and his father's been shoveling coal since the start of our great age of industry."

Blaney, freckle-faced, curly-haired, and thin, nodded and drank from the brown bottle before him.

"A model family," Patrick's mother added, "the kind of men who make Belfast proud."

"Martin here has been across the Atlantic six times, and he isn't yet twenty years old."

"You've been eight, though, haven't you James?" Patrick asked.

"And starting tomorrow, nine!" James declared. "Crossing the ocean on the grandest ship of all."

So it was true! His brother was actually sailing on *Titanic*. Like most people in Belfast, Patrick already knew all the facts about the boat they called the Queen of the Sea: Nearly nine hundred feet long, nearly one hundred feet wide, one hundred fifty-nine coal burning furnaces, twenty-nine boilers. And she was built right there in Belfast: Patrick had gone to see her up close more than once. Her iron-plated bow stood forward with such confidence, force, and power that she looked capable of steaming right through the heart of the city, pushing aside its buildings and carving a new river in her wake.

"God bless you and *Titanic*," his mother said, her face alight with pride.

Someday, Patrick hoped, she'd look at him that way.

"The sea trials begin at six tomorrow morning," James said. "They say half the city will be there to watch."

"They should! She's the pride of Belfast," his mother added.

"And we are the wind in her sails, stoking the fires that turn her turbines and give her speed."

"Here's to the Black Gang," Blaney added. "She'd be no more than a barge without us shoveling that coal!"

Prompted by his mother's stare, Patrick fetched a few new

bottles. When he returned, Blaney pointed to the now empty bookshelf against the wall. "Planning to start a library, are you?"

"No, no!" his mother said. "We've only now rid ourselves of one, thanks be to God. I'll have no son of mine burying his head in fantasies and fairy tales like their father. My sons are workers. Isn't that right James?"

Patrick hoped his mother didn't go on. She talked about his father like he was some neighborhood drunk. She viciously mocked his failed dreams—a plan to build the first movie house in Belfast was a favorite target—and his love of books.

"If my own husband was a worker, I would be in a respectable house, not this shrunken cave," she said.

Blaney removed a watch from the pocket of his woolen vest, and showed James the time.

They were leaving. Patrick watched his mother's face lose its color.

"You won't stay the night?" she asked.

"We start our work at just past four in the morning, mother. It's better we board now, catch a few hours sleep in the bunks."

"To be sure, to be sure," she said sadly.

Blaney pushed back from the table and stood up first, holding a tattered woolen cap in his hands. "Thank you kindly, Mrs. Waters."

James wrapped their mother in a powerful hug.

"If I'm to honor the Waters name, I shouldn't be sitting around this table now, should I?" James asked.

"Come down and watch her if you can," Blaney said to Patrick. "See that black smoke rushing out of the stacks and think of us."

His mother pressed James's hand. "You'll come back soon?"

"You won't even know we were gone," James said. "We'll be to America and back before the end of the month."

A VERY, VERY POOR IDEA

Patrick's mother woke him with two kicks to his mattress and her regular morning greeting. "Up! You're not staying in a fine hotel!"

As she reminded him daily, his father was a loafer, a man who sat about thinking all day, and whose thinking only brought them debts, death, and heartache. Her sons would not turn out that way. They would be real men who stayed on their feet until they were too tired to stand. This was her cause for taking him out of school the year before and marching him around the city until he secured a job. His former classmates were playing ball and making faces behind Father Conmee's back, but Patrick was no longer spoiled by boyhood. The time had come for him to be a man, and he had accepted the challenge.

He rubbed his face with his hands, flattened his large ears, and roughly scratched his head.

In the kitchen, his mother stood with her back to the small stove, holding a wooden spoon at her side. She stared blankly across the room.

"What is it?" he asked.

"The test runs were cancelled on account of high winds."

Smoke wafted up behind her. She cursed and grabbed the pot off the stove, then dropped it on the counter and sucked the underside of a finger. "And now I've gone and burned your porridge."

Patrick put a hand on her shoulder, but she shrugged him away. This would not be a good day for his mother; he could see the dark cloud forming, her shoulders slacking. He moved the pot of porridge to the sink, drank down a glass of milk, grabbed a hunk of thick brown bread, and kissed her on her cold, pale cheek. A year ago he would have had to stand up on his toes, but now he actually had to lean down. "I'm off," he said.

Outside, Belfast was busier than usual, even for a Monday. The whole city had come out to watch *Titanic* and the strong, heavy smell of coal filled the air. After a few breaths, gritty black dust coated his tongue. The taste of progress, as Mr. Joyce called it.

Hands digging into the pockets of his wool jacket, Patrick walked with his eyes low and chin tucked in toward his chest. The way working men walked.

He approached O'Neill's through the narrow, wet alley at the back, kicked his boots against the stone wall, then wiped them on the straw mat.

The kitchen was clean when he left the night before, but now the glasses were piled high, and he heard far more noise inside than usual. It sounded like the end of the day, not the start.

He pushed through the swinging door to let Mr. Joyce know he'd arrived and immediately saw James, Martin Blaney, and five other men. Most were at least a decade older than his brother and thin, with coal-dusted faces framing bright white eyes.

"There he is!" James declared.

Mr. Joyce was surprised but pleased to see Patrick so early.

"High winds," James explained, "so we were given a few hours of daylight before returning to the bowels of the queen."

"And look what we've chosen instead of daylight," said one of the older men. "From one cave to another."

"Are you here for chatter or work?" Mr. Joyce asked.

James took Patrick by the shoulders and turned him to face the proprietor. "Waters men are workers! What needs to be done?"

A great deal of work needed to be done, in fact, and the hours passed quickly. The men soon turned to singing songs of the sea and of love. Eventually James came into the kitchen to say good-bye. "We're going to the ship, leaving tomorrow," he said. "I'll send you a note from New York!"

James hugged Patrick, then walloped him on the shoulder with one of his big, gnarled fists, hard enough to leave a bruise, and raced out.

The pub gradually filled with rowdy, red-faced men. Normally Mondays were quiet, but one of the patrons was leading the rest in song. He stood atop a table to conduct the others, slipped in a small puddle of beer, and fell to the floor.

Mr. Joyce glanced at Patrick and nodded in the direction of the fallen singer. Patrick hurried over and helped the man into a seat. He recognized him now. The singer had been sitting with James earlier in the day.

The man wiped his brow with a small piece of paper, then slapped it down on the table. A *Titanic* work slip!

Patrick stared into the man's glassy eyes. "Are you supposed to be on the boat?" he asked.

"She'll wait for John McGuinness," the man boasted. "I'm the finest trimmer in Belfast." With one eyebrow arched, McGuinness raised a finger in the air as if he were about to say something profound. But his head dropped to the table before he could utter a word. One of the men across the table reached for the slip, but Patrick grabbed it first and shoved it in his pocket. The man clasped Patrick's shoulder, but Mr. Joyce was up and over the bar in seconds. "Easy now," he said, and the man released his grip.

Mr. Joyce grabbed a clump of McGuinness's curls and gently

lifted his head. His eyes were lifeless. "He won't be moving for a half a day or more."

"But he's supposed to report to *Titanic*."

"That is not our problem, Patrick. He was granted the privilege, and now he has squandered that chance. *Titanic* won't miss him. They'll find another man to fill his place."

What a terrible waste! A right-minded man would do anything for the chance to work on that magnificent ship. Patrick thrust his hands into his pockets and felt the work slip.

There was one other choice.

He pulled out the paper. The ticket merely bore the White Star Line logo, the ship's name, and the words: "Admit one crew." And yes, the ticket belonged to this man, John McGuinness, but his name wasn't actually printed on it, and he certainly was in no condition to use it. They'd give his job to another trimmer, a stranger. Which meant that James might have a stranger working by his side. And James did not deserve that. If James was going to help *Titanic* master the ocean, he would need a friend working by his side. A brother.

"Give that here," yelled the man who'd tried to grab the ticket. "I need the work. I'm as strong a trimmer as this bloke."

Patrick closed the paper in his hands and faced Mr. Joyce. He tried to stand taller.

"Oh, no," said Mr. Joyce. "That is a very, very poor idea."

"I'm tall enough," Patrick replied.

"You haven't a wisp of hair on your chin."

"I'm strong."

"For a woman."

"Even if I'm not old enough or strong enough or hairy enough, you're the one who says a man must associate himself with greatness. How many more chances like this will I have?"

Mr. Joyce returned to the bar. A minute must have passed, perhaps two, before he reached into the till, removed some bills, folded them and tucked them into Patrick's pocket. Next he pulled a worn woolen cap off a hook and placed it on Patrick's head. "Your wages and your new cap. Keep it low, and your voice lower when you board that boat. I'll send word to your mother."

Patrick stood there, frozen.

"Off with you, boy! Off to *Titanic*!"

SIR FRANCIS BACON'S SECRET

The Dorchester, a lushly upholstered hotel in the center of London, entertained only the most privileged guests. The restaurant in particular was no place for the working-man. The staff was outfitted in the finest uniforms and conducted themselves with flawless charm and grace. Paintings worthy of the finest museums hung from the walls. Splendid drapes and tapestries adorned the room, and the tables were set for royalty. A setting of silver alone would fetch enough money to pay several months of Berryman's rent.

Yet he was not there to steal. He was there, seated at a table in the very center of the main dining room, because he had an appointment with a guest of the hotel, Mr. Archibald Rockwell. The very man who recruited him to the quest for Sir Francis Bacon's secret. Berryman first met Mr. Rockwell at the college, when the huge man, nearly spherical in shape, burst out of Professor Horgan's office red-faced with frustration.

Berryman had been standing outside the door, listening to their exchange with interest. He learned that Mr. Rockwell was engaged in a kind of treasure hunt involving the great Sir Francis Bacon and that he had come to Horgan, a noted expert on the man, for insight.

Of course, the decrepit, stubborn Horgan dismissed him. He said that he had already wasted too much time in his life patiently listening to wild-eyed amateurs propound fantastic theories about Sir Francis Bacon. He would not stand another.

As Mr. Rockwell burst angrily from the office, Berryman deftly bumped him, apologized, and asked if perhaps he could offer assistance. He had a sharp mind and a formidable memory, he said, and he demonstrated the latter by loosely quoting a line from the *Essaies*.

"*Glorious men are the scorn of wise men*," he began, "*the admiration of fools, the idols of parasites, and the slaves of their own vaunts.*"

"A fitting quote," Mr. Rockwell replied. "That was no gentleman. You are a student here?"

"A reader," Berryman answered. In truth he had hoped to achieve that position, perhaps in a year or two. At the time he was merely conducting research for several different professors.

Mr. Rockwell fingered his very thick mustache and pulled his waistband up around his large stomach. From the pocket of his coat he produced a small, golden-crusted roll and hungrily bit off a chunk. "You overheard my queries?" he asked as he chewed.

"I did," Mr. Berryman replied, "and I believe I can help you. I know Bacon as well as old Horgan, yet I also possess a special set of skills which might prove useful in your quest."

With little ceremony he handed Mr. Rockwell the wallet he had just lifted from the man's coat.

Mr. Rockwell smiled as though he were staring at a particularly appetizing meal. "Yes," he said, "yes, indeed."

And thus their partnership was formed.

Now, two years later, after Berryman had conducted countless hours of research and completed a dozen expert thefts from private libraries, book dealers, and college archives, Mr. Rockwell was smiling once more.

Berryman saw him the moment he entered, for he was a hard man to miss. He leaned back as he walked, steering his stomach between the tables like a coachman directing a team of horses. His manners, though, were unfortunately American. Even from a distance Mr. Berryman could see something small and yellowish stuck to one of his plump cheeks. He seemed incapable of eating without leaving some trace of the food on his face.

Though Mr. Rockwell's presentation was lacking, Berryman was relieved at his arrival. He had felt the other guests and patrons watching him, waiting there alone at the table, as if they knew he did not truly belong among them. As if they could smell his debts. But now they would see that he was there for an important meeting.

Soon, in fact, he would be one of them. If Berryman and Rockwell's theory about what Bacon had hidden inside that little book proved correct, the silver on the table before him would carry no more value than a simple wrench. They believed that the great Francis Bacon had uncovered the secret of alchemy, the power to transform any base metal into gold through chemistry. Furthermore, they had evidence to suggest that Bacon had hidden this recipe for boundless wealth in one particular copy of his *Essaies*—the very same copy that Quaritch had sold to Harry Widener. All they had to do was procure the book and find the formula within it. Then Berryman's debts would vanish like bubbles popped in flight.

He would be a modern Midas.

Mr. Rockwell deposited himself opposite Berryman. "Don't delay man!" Mr. Rockwell said. "Let me see it!"

Fixated on the small piece of food stuck to his face, which he now saw was a fleck of greasy, roasted chicken skin, Berryman paused before replying. "No, you misunderstood me. I don't have the book. I merely wrote to you that I'd found it. You see, I learned that Bernard Quaritch, the bookseller, had procured . . ."

He let his words trail off. Mr. Rockwell's face was as red as an apple.

Through clenched teeth he replied, "You told me you'd found it. Naturally I assumed, when you requested this meeting, that you would bring it with you."

"No, I told you I knew where it was—"

"My patience is exhausted, Berryman. I want that book now. No matter the cost."

Two women about his age sauntered by and caught Berryman's eye. They whispered to each other; had they noticed his clothes? His suit was clearly not custom-tailored.

"Mr. Berryman!"

"Yes . . . I understand. I discovered that the copy is now in the hands of Harry Elkins Widener, coincidentally a classmate of mine at Harvard—"

"I know the Widener family, Berryman. Where is he?"

"He left London for France a few days ago, but will return to America aboard the new ocean liner *Titanic*."

Mr. Rockwell brightened. "Wonderful."

A waiter strutted past bearing a crystal bowl packed with celery, carrot sticks, and radishes. With surprising quickness Mr. Rockwell reached out and pulled the thickest of the carrots from the bowl and snapped off one end in his mouth.

"Wonderful? But he's leaving, sir . . ."

"So am I, Berryman. I booked my passage home on that ship several weeks ago. Hmmmm . . . this turn of events is quite delicious; though of course we will have to devise a way to get you aboard."

"Me, sir? On *Titanic*?"

The luck! Finally Fortune was smiling upon him. He'd have to find a new suit, something to wear to dinner. He'd show them all that he belonged.

"Of course there will be no tickets available in first class."

"No?"

After snapping off another hunk of carrot, Mr. Rockwell formed a rectangle with his fingers and thumbs, closed one eye, and peered through the gap as if he were a painter framing Berryman for a portrait.

His face was thoughtfully contorted when he asked, "Are you a flexible man, Mr. Berryman?"

CITY OF IRON AND STEEL

The damp street was pockmarked with gray puddles, and most of Belfast was sleeping. Patrick should have been sleeping, too. Really, what was he doing? They'd never allow him on that ship.

His forehead itched furiously; he'd pulled the rim of the coarse wool cap down nearly to his eyebrows. At Queen's Road he spotted her looming in the distance. She was a mountain! A self-contained city of iron and steel: eight hundred and eighty feet long. Nearly two hundred feet tall. More than four hundred thousand rivets. How could she even float?

A hand clapped him lightly on the back. A large, white-mustached old man stood staring with him. "Have a good look, boy, she'll be gone in the morning."

Patrick nodded, resumed walking. Boy! The old man called

him a boy because he had stopped to stare in wonder like one. He adjusted his cap and scolded himself.

A gangway ran from the dock through a small door in *Titanic's* hull, like a drawbridge leading into a castle. The rest of the city might have felt deserted, but here he found a lively, thick, angry cluster of men, all smoking and shouting for work.

"Why does a Belfast-built boat need an English crew?"

"A Belfast boat should be run by Belfast men!"

A lone officer stood listening at the other end of the ramp, a step inside the ship, holding a list and a pencil. "If you're not here as crew, I can do you no favors," he said.

As Patrick moved closer, a man who smelled as though he'd never even heard of a bath elbowed him aside. Patrick stumbled, nearly fell into a puddle of muddied water. "Out of the way!" the man yelled.

But Patrick was not someone to be pushed aside. Not even by a man with twice his girth. He adjusted his cap, tested his deep delivery—*John McGuinness, John McGuinness*—then bumped and angled his way through the men and straight up the gangway.

Black water lay below him in the gap between boat and dock; fear seized his throat and chest. He could swim well. His father had taught him. Yet there was something about this ship, and the black water below.

"Name?"

"Mc . . . Guinness," he mumbled, handing the man the slip. "John McGuinness."

"Again? Speak up!"

Back straight, chin tucked, cap low, he growled, "John Mc-Guinness."

The officer reviewed his list and checked off the name. Behind Patrick, the men yelled in protest, but he moved forward. He had one foot on the boat, in fact, when the officer stopped him. He placed the tip of his pencil under Patrick's chin and pushed upward. "Says here you're one and twenty years old, but you have the voice and face of a schoolboy."

Patrick grimaced. If he didn't look like a trimmer, he would have to talk like one. "Maybe so," he answered back, recalling something he'd heard his brother say, "but my blood runs black from the coal I've been shoveling these five years."

The officer looked beyond him for a moment. "McGuinness . . . I know the name. I thought he was the bois-terous fellow. The one who's always singing."

"No, you're thinking of Joyce," Patrick blurted, using the first name that came to him.

Behind him, the men were becoming increasingly rowdy. He faked a dry, heaving cough and borrowed a few more phrases he'd heard the last two days. "Now if you'll kindly let me pass, I'll be getting back to my boys in the Black Gang. This fresh air is no good for a trimmer's lungs."

The officer lowered his list. "In with you now. Sorry for the trouble."

And in Patrick went, into the great ship as fast as he could walk. But where? The halls were high-ceilinged, freshly painted white, and wider than he would have guessed. He hurried, hoping to put some distance between himself and the gangway. He ascended several flights of stairs and stepped into a perfectly white hallway with a thick, mostly red carpet. The carpet was softer underfoot than damp green moss. The hall was lined with doors, each of which bore an ivory plaque inscribed with a number. Would one of those rooms be his?

Two uniformed, broad-faced men appeared at the far end of the hall.

"What are you doing, boy?" one of them called.

"These are the first class cabins. You could be thrown off the ship for being up here," said the other.

"Sorry, I lost my way," Patrick said. "I'm a trimmer."

"Then you better get down to the boilers before you sully these halls."

"Thank you . . . yes . . . and how would I get there?"

The bearded man pointed to a door. "Through there and down. Just follow the noise."

"And the heat."

"Aye, and the smell."

The door led through to a stairway that reached into the

very depths of the boat. A deep rumbling grew louder with every few steps. His boots clanged on the metal stairs. He heard the engines not merely with his ears, but with the whole of his body. The vibrations pulsed along every inch of him, up through his feet to his spine, the base of his ears, his jaw.

The harsh smell of burning coal began to thicken the air. He could taste the fine grit, feel it on his tongue. He knew he was getting closer to James. He'd surprise his brother—show him that he was no longer just a boy. They might even work side by side! Two Waters men, powering the greatest ship man had ever known!

The rumbling and growling intensified, and at the bottom of the stairs Patrick found himself in what had to be the engine room. Years before, when he was eight or nine, his father had shown him the engine of an automobile, and now he felt like he'd been shrunk to the size of a bug and left to wander around inside that great machine. Everything was enormous. The engines were the size of his house. Great pipes snaked and threaded in every direction overhead. He had entered the sweltering, dark, noisy heart of the ship—his brother's home.

An official-looking member of the crew approached him with a list. This time, Patrick allowed the man no chance to ask a question. "Where would I find James Waters?"

"Boiler room five. Through those doors there," he said, pointing behind him.

Through a steel-framed doorway in the monstrous wall ahead of him Patrick could see a series of identical doors beyond. He stepped through the first one, past more massive engines, hurried down a narrow passageway, came to a corner, and found trimmers and stokers working busily to his right and left.

The huge, black coal bunkers were on one side, the fiery boilers on the other, and the spaces between them were cramped, hot as an open fire, and ear-bursting loud. The aisle was packed with red, coal-covered, sweating men, and through the open mouths of the boilers he saw the orange hellfire of burning coals. The men jammed heavy iron rods and shovels deep into those fiery throats, undaunted by the heat. James was not among them.

A burly trimmer handling a wheelbarrow cast him a bothered glance, so Patrick stepped through the next doorway. The less attention he attracted, the better.

Patrick crossed through three more of the doorways into the fifth room. There, at last, he found his brother and Blaney working next to one another, shoveling and leveling coal through an opening in a great steel bunker.

"James!" he shouted, but his brother heard nothing.

Patrick dodged between a few other men and punched him in the arm. His fist glanced off his brother's sweating shoulder.

James turned burning white eyes on him. His skin was red where it wasn't smeared with black. He dropped his tool, an iron rod, and it bounced heavily against the floor. "Patrick? What are you doing here?"

"I thought . . . I tried . . . ," Patrick began.

"You didn't sneak aboard, did you?" James pressed his hand to his sweating forehead. "They'll throw us both off at Southampton if you did!"

"No! I'm here to work," Patrick explained. He decided it would be better to leave out McGuinness.

"Work? Where?"

"Right here," Patrick answered. But he could see that his brother was not pleased.

Blaney pulled James aside to talk. The deep thump of the turbines, the underlying hiss of the burning coal, the sporadic bursts of steam and a hundred other little noises prevented Patrick from hearing a word.

His brother's reaction was inexplicable. James should have been proud. James should have congratulated him!

Blaney picked up his shovel and turned back to the bunker. Grimacing, James wiped his soaked face with a coal-smudged rag, and inspected his younger brother. "I don't see how a scrawny, milk-fed, book-bred boy like my little brother is going to survive down here, but Blaney says I ought to give you a chance."

Patrick pulled off his cap and rushed at James. "Thank you! Thank you!"

"Save your energy," James said. He coughed; another deep,

chest-shaking rumble. "If you can't prove yourself up to the task, I can't save this job for you, and I won't want to. If you can't do your share, that's more work for myself, Martin, and the rest."

A short, muscled and mustached trimmer rolled up an empty wheelbarrow. His arms looked hard as steel. As James shoveled in coal from the bunker, Blaney leveled what remained.

"This bunker is storage, see?" James yelled over his shoulder. "The coal from here goes into this cart and then Mr. Hendrickson here"—the man pushed the now-full wheelbarrow away —"moves it over to the furnace."

Patrick appreciated the thought, but James had already told him all about the work of a trimmer, and he'd heard the men at O'Neill's discuss how the great, coal-fueled oceanliners made such speed. Before James could go on, Patrick said, "And the coal in the furnace keeps the boilers burning hot, producing the steam that spins the turbines and turns the propellers."

Blaney punched James, smiling. "Impressive!"

"It's not his brains I'm worried about," James said. "It's his back."

Patrick tossed his cap and jacket aside. He'd seen enough. He could do it himself, and he would start right then to extinguish his brother's doubts. "Let me try," he said.

"You can watch for now. We do four hours on and eight off. John's shift . . . your shift now, I guess . . . doesn't start until midnight.

Patrick pulled the shovel away from his brother. "Then we'll consider the next few hours a training period."

"Very well, little brother," James said. "Start training."

For a moment Patrick watched the way Blaney gripped the shovel, studied the spacing between his hands. Hendrickson appeared with another empty cart and Patrick did his best to copy what his brother had done.

Resting against the wall, James offered the occasional compliment—"Nice form" or "Good pace"—and a few hints. He reminded him to use his legs, not his arms, and to loosen his grip so his hands wouldn't tire too quickly.

Unfortunately, Patrick was soon exhausted. After five minutes he needed to stop and shake his searing hot, cramping hands. Ten minutes later he could have quit for the day, but his brother was still watching him; and Blaney, like a machine, hadn't stopped once.

So, Patrick kept going: shoveling, leveling, trimming. He'd never felt such heat. He was drenched with sweat, as though he'd taken a bath in his clothes. His feet were sweating straight through his socks, soaking his boots.

His eyes were burning and bleary. Too many times already he'd mistakenly tried to rub them clear of sweat with coal-stained hands.

Patrick decided that hell itself wouldn't be this hot. He thought of one of his father's favorite stories, the *Inferno*, about a poet who wanders through the underworld. He remembered how they'd sit together, at night, and his father would read this story, or one of his other favorites, aloud.

The memory of his father spurred him on to work even harder. Patrick wasn't going to end up dead and disrespected at an early age. He was going to restore the Waters name. He and James, working side by side, were going to power the world's greatest ocean liner across the Atlantic.

"Not too fast now," Blaney warned. "You still have hours to go."

But Patrick wasn't going to hear it. He was young. He was strong. He would be the best trimmer they had, as good or better than his brother.

Those fires began burning within him, as if he were part of the engine itself. He worked faster and faster. A tingling sensation arose in his hands and feet. His stomach grew queasy. But he kept at his task. Except for his boiling face, he wasn't even hot anymore. His head had begun to feel cool.

He must have been an impressive sight, for Blaney stopped and began to stare. Then Patrick heard his brother call him, watched the room upend itself, and felt someone grab his arms.

TO BE PROPERLY DRESSED

Wrapped in a woolen blanket, John Francis Berryman sat at the lone table in his unfortunately small room and surveyed once more what he had set out for the voyage. The varied items were neatly arrayed before him. The blond wig with its thick curls. The short blond mustache to match. The large and far more prominent brown mustache and the accompanying rubber nose. The makeup case that enabled him to render this bulbous prosthetic a seamless addition to his face. Yes, these were all good choices.

There were shoes and heel extensions to make him a taller man. Padding that would add thickness to his midsection. He included several pairs of spectacles, the lenses of which had been replaced with glass. And of course, in the center of it all, three neatly folded replicas of the uniforms which first class stewards and waiters would wear aboard the ship.

His book knife lay wrapped inside an old scarf. The knife, really, was the reason for the third uniform. There was a very good chance he would have to use the blade on someone— perhaps even Widener himself—and he imagined that a victim's blood would have no respect for a steward's white jacket. The thinnest and briefest of streams would undoubtedly imprint a permanent stain. If he had secured only two of the uniforms, and one was marred by blood, then he would be forced to wear the remaining one repeatedly. This, of course, would be unacceptable.

Berryman was impressed with his own preparedness, yet the sight of those uniforms, and the thought that he'd have to wear them, was terribly offensive. He was not meant to serve those passengers. He belonged among them!

Of course, he did understand Mr. Rockwell's logic. In the service of their quest, this was the most sensible course of action. He would be allowed to move more freely about the ship by posing as a member of the staff.

A cup of tea sat before him; he sipped from it carefully and decided that he would pack the dinner jacket after all. Mr. Rockwell might protest, but what if they revealed the formula during the voyage? What if they began transforming base metals into gold immediately, and he arrived in New York a suddenly and fabulously wealthy man? He'd take the finest suite in the finest hotel, of course, one with closets larger than his current, incurably small room, but he wouldn't want to enter one of those palaces in the clothes of a common man. He'd want to be properly dressed.

His current lodgings were far from luxurious. Berryman winced at the sight of his reading chair, with its stained cushions and chipped wood frame, and the frayed sheets spread across his bed. And the cold in the room! The blanket wrapped around his back and shoulders hardly kept out the damp London chill, which was sucking the heat from his tea. He drank the last of it quickly and once more surveyed the items before him. Several days remained until his departure, but he really had packed perfectly. He could think of nothing else, nothing he'd forgotten.

In a few days he would drop his valise at the Dorchester, and Mr. Rockwell would take it aboard along with his own luggage. He had arranged to sneak Berryman onto *Titanic* through some other means; something that required flexibility, apparently. Berryman wasn't certain he'd like the method, but he believed firmly that securing the book would be worth whatever minor hardship he had to endure.

THE DEMIGOD OF SPIT

Patrick opened his eyes to a view of a paneled white ceiling. His clothes were cold and damp. His shoes and socks had been pulled off, and he was in a large room packed tightly with wood-framed bunks, lying on one of the upper beds.

"Good morning," James said. "How do you feel?"

Patrick rolled to his side, closed and reopened his eyes. Morning? He had a vague, dreamlike memory of waking on the floor of the boiler room, then being carried up several flights of stairs and tossed here. He did not feel well. Not at all.

James moved to a washbasin, opened the faucet, and held a towel under the stream, then passed it to his brother. "Cold, fresh seawater," he said.

Patrick ran the icy towel across his forehead, his eyes, the back of his neck. His feet tingled, but felt cool, and his stomach was roiling with bile. A terrible metallic taste filled his mouth, as if he'd been sucking on a coin.

Yet none of these sensations matched the strong, sickening swell of disappointment. "The heat," he began. "I didn't know . . . I hadn't eaten enough . . ."

"Father was a fainter, too," James said. "Did you know that? Fainted on his wedding day. He was waiting for Mother on the altar at St. Michael's, dressed in his sharpest tweed suit, when a spell of nerves came over him, and he dropped right to the floor. Uncle John had to rouse him. Splashed a whole bowl of holy water on his face, I heard, which made Father Conmee howling mad."

The two brothers laughed. The towel, the story, the joke: These were his brother's ways of telling Patrick that he had not ruined the situation completely. But the Black Gang, Patrick guessed, would not welcome him back.

"What now?" Patrick asked.

"Well, she has left the dock for her sea trials, so there will be no going back to Belfast now. Yet I won't have you back in the boiler room, either. I found another position for you. Something more suited to your gentle nature."

Slowly, Patrick lowered himself to the cold floor. His head washed about as if his brain were floating on the waves. "What is it?"

"I don't know exactly, but you're to be part of the waitstaff."

Patrick clenched his teeth. This was a step back! A major retreat. He wanted to work, not wait on people.

"It was the only one I could find," James explained. "Another man failed the health inspection. Lice, you know?"

"But I want a *real* job. A man's job. I'll end up washing dirty glasses all day."

James smiled. "Yes, but you'll be washing dirty glasses on *Titanic*."

He had no choice. Patrick guessed that if he declined this position, he'd be forced to disembark at the next port. That would be far worse. If he couldn't work with the Black Gang, he would show them that he could be of some value to the ship.

"On to the dishware then," he said, and he tossed the soaked towel at his brother's face.

James wiped his face and made for the door. "You'll report to Mr. Webb. If he asks, you have five years experience in Belfast's finest pubs. He'll be on D Deck, I imagine, near the First-Class Dining Room. Look for a stiff, strong man with a thick neck."

"How do I get to D Deck?"

"It would be one deck above this one, but how you'd get there I have no idea," James laughed. "If I don't hear from you in a day or two, I'll send help."

Patrick wasn't lost for a day, but it felt nearly that long. Eventually he found himself crossing an outdoor deck, heading toward the stern. The sky was bright enough that he had to squint.

Belfast was visible over the rails. He'd never looked down on the city from such a height, but he dared not stop for long. His new boss was expecting him.

Patrick hurried up another flight of stairs, pushed through a revolving door, entered the empty passenger halls, and came to a grand, winding staircase. The woodwork, the gloss of the varnish, the sweep of the banisters as they descended, flowing toward the base—all of it was mesmerizing. Oh, to slide down that rail. The speed he'd gain!

Now would be the time, given that the room would belong to the passengers in a matter of days, but when Patrick turned to see if anyone was watching, he noticed two uniformed men walking his way. He took the carpeted stairs one step at a time, and soon spotted a stiff, thick-necked man standing in a doorway, staring into a vast dining hall. Mr. Webb, he guessed.

Patrick approached quietly, studying the room beyond. A hundred or more tables had to be spread throughout the space. Great glass chandeliers hung from the ornately paneled ceilings. Light filled the room, streaming in through large windows, some of which were clear, some red and blue and yellow stained glass.

Mr. Webb turned to face him. "Mr. Waters?"

"Yes, sir," Patrick said, stepping into the room.

"Your brother says you have training."

"Five years, sir, in some of the finest pubs in Belfast."

Mr. Webb studied him and Patrick did the same. He had the neck and jaw of a dockworker, a man who hauled beams and barrels all day. His head, square and flat on top, looked like it had been riveted to his shoulders. His collar was stiff, high, and tight around his neck. Everything about him was heavy and hard, including his stare. "There are no fine pubs in Belfast, Mr. Waters, and I would guess, by the look of you, that you haven't been working for more than a year."

After a pause Patrick admitted, "Eighteen months, sir. And the pub was a rotten, moldy place, but I kept the pint glasses clean and dry."

Mr. Webb's thin lips stretched across his hardened face. "Good! Honesty will serve you well with me, Mr. Waters. But not with the passengers. You'll tell them you are seventeen years of age."

"Of course."

"And you'll need to scrub yourself clean of coal dust," he said. "I smell the fire on you still."

Walking ahead, Mr. Webb pushed on one of the tables as they crossed the room. It did not budge.

"I haven't been down yet myself, but I've heard her engines are a marvel. I have real respect for your brother and the rest of the Black Gang. Was it impossibly hot?"

"Yes, sir, hot as the seventh—"

Patrick stopped himself. He'd sound like his father, with talk like that.

"The seventh what?" Mr. Webb asked.

"Nothing."

"The seventh circle of hell, perhaps?" he said with a smile. "Do you know Dante, Mr. Waters?"

"A little."

"Very impressive for a boy your age. Very impressive, indeed. But I'll have to ask you to refrain from referring to epic poems for the remainder of our journey. We can't have the passengers thinking that a dishwasher is as educated as they are. Our job is to make them feel utterly, completely superior."

Mr. Webb quickened his pace across the bright blue and red carpet. Patrick recalled that he hadn't cleaned his boots, but thankfully he wasn't leaving any coal-dust footprints.

A pair of wide, leather-encased doors separated the dining saloon from the galley, a maze of halls and closets crowded with shining stovetops and steel counters, sinks and massive ovens. Pots large enough to boil a pig whole hung from hooks overhead. At O'Neill's alehouse, there were never more than two people in the kitchen, but Mr. Webb said forty or fifty men would be rushing around inside the space. Patrick imagined them bouncing off one another, like a single billiards table hosting five games at once.

As they walked, Mr. Webb pointed to rooms on his left and right, calling out, "Oysters in here . . . the scullery is that way . . . vegetables will be prepared for cooking in the room to your left."

Inside a small room off a narrow hall, a long shelf was stacked entirely with silver spittoons. Mr. Webb pulled one down. "The first class lounges will have spittoons, like this one, placed throughout. You will empty them, wash them out, and return them to their proper place. You will also collect any other dirtied plates, crystal, demitasse cups, china, or silverware that you find."

They strode through the galley and Mr. Webb took the spittoon with him. He stopped, tilted his chin up, his head back, and breathed in powerfully through his nose, loosening something thick and wet. With a grunt and a grimace he spat it into the silver basin, producing a surprisingly loud ding. "This spittoon, and its brethren, will be your chief responsibility. You will become unusually familiar with spit, Mr. Waters. You will be an expert in spit. An arbiter. You will be the demigod of spit on this ship."

"The demigod, sir?" Patrick asked.

Mr. Webb ignored his question and walked ahead. Enjoying the tour, Patrick joined his hands behind his back; his father used to walk that way. The pose annoyed his mother, though, and Mr. Webb was not fond of it either.

"We are not strolling a sculpture garden, Mr. Waters! Hands at your sides, eyes forward, please. And keep your back straight. You slouch like a parched flower."

Patrick stood up, thrust his shoulders back. "Like this?"

"Yes, much improved. Appearance is paramount! We are here to serve, not to stroll, and we must look that way at all times."

Mr. Webb knocked on the wall to their left. "Through here is the hospital," he said, "though the entrance is above us on C Deck."

Next they moved through a wide pantry, emerged in another hall, and turned right.

"Which way are we walking now, Mr. Waters? Astern?"

"No, sir," Patrick replied. They had turned right, and right again. "I believe we're heading abow."

"There's no such term, Mr. Waters, but I applaud your effort, and we are, in fact, walking toward the bow. It is important that you learn your way around this ship. She is something of a labyrinth."

A thin steward with wide hips was pushing a cart laden with small wooden boxes across the passageway. Mr. Webb, raising his eyebrows, held out the spittoon. The steward sucked and swished and ejected a yellowish stream into the bottom.

"Thank you, Mr. Moore," he said, then marched across the galley again, through another swinging door, and over to a narrow set of stairs. Patrick had to race to keep pace. They sped up three flights. He grew dizzy; the effects of the fainting had not entirely cleared.

"This is A Deck," Webb said at the top. "The Boat Deck is the uppermost, then A, B, and so on, down to the Tank Top Deck, where your brother and his boys toil. A Deck will be your new home."

The stairs led to a smaller but hardly insignificant pantry. Rows and rows of shelves were stacked with china, silver, and crystal alongside clean linens, countless spittoons, and small wooden boxes containing every brand and type of tobacco. The room was nearly empty now, with only two men inside unloading boxes of china, but Patrick could imagine the coming chaos.

A short, freckled waiter with a thin mustache passed by them on his way out the door. Mr. Webb extended the spittoon and the man coughed out a small comet of spittle.

From the pantry they walked to the First-Class Smoking Room, a dark, wood-paneled space made for men. Patrick immediately knew that this would be his favorite room on *Titanic*. The deep brown wood, the yellowish light from the electric lamps, and the thick many-colored rugs all felt somehow right to him. The chairs were all deep green leather, the furniture carved from hard, finely-grained mahogany by Irish craftsmen of the highest skill.

Mr. Webb led him to a square wooden table with a cast iron base. "Go ahead, pick it up," he said.

Patrick grabbed the edges and lifted. Nothing: The legs were bolted to the floor. "In case of high seas," Mr. Webb explained. "And do you notice the edge?" He took a glass, placed it in the center, and slid it towards one side. It hit a raised rim and stopped. "Again, in case of high seas: not a drink will be spilled."

Mr. Webb held up a finger and looked at him directly. "Everything to the highest standard, everything thought of in advance, Mr. Waters."

"Is this where I'll be working?"

"That is undecided. But your universe will be centered in part on these spittoons, Mr. Waters, and this room will be the center of spittoon activity, so you will at the very least pass through here frequently to collect the expectorations of these great men."

"Expectorations, sir?"

"Their spit, Mr. Waters. The yellow, green, brown, sinewy refuse of their tobacco-filled maws."

Patrick nodded begrudgingly. The fiery boiler rooms were suddenly appealing.

RAVENOUS MR. ROCKWELL

On the morning of Wednesday, April 10, Archibald Rockwell endured a terrible misfortune. An ignorant Dorchester Hotel concierge had somehow misplaced his instructions to arrange for a first class seat on the boat train to Southampton and he was forced to sit with the rabble instead. A single second-class seat was all that remained, and he had no choice but to take it. Otherwise he would miss *Titanic*'s departure.

Despite his predicament, Archibald Rockwell was in no way second-class. His cunning, he believed, was renowned, and his business acumen, if you asked him, was admired in boardrooms across America. Yet there he was, lodged in an uncomfortably small seat, mired amid the masses.

He comforted himself with three facts. First, by offering an almost presentable young man a few pounds to vacate the spot, he had procured a window seat. The journey from London's Waterloo Station to *Titanic*'s dock in Southampton was two hours long and the views of the green English countryside would be pleasing enough to occupy his demanding mind for a significant portion of the time. By staring out the window, he could also pretend that he did not hear the woman next to him, who on several occasions attempted to initiate a conversation.

The second pleasing fact was the presence of numerous small sandwiches stored in the pockets of his coat. When the Dorchester manager had apologized for his employee's mistake, and asked how he could compensate Mr. Rockwell for his troubles, he replied, "In sandwiches!"

Though surprised at first, the manager complied, supplying him with a delightful assortment.

Third, and finally, he could always remind himself that Berryman was much worse off. At least Mr. Rockwell had a seat on the train and a ticket on the ship herself. Berryman, on the other hand, was currently riding in the baggage car, stuffed inside a very large trunk. Mr. Rockwell himself had poked it full of numerous holes so that his resourceful associate would be able to breathe. He reluctantly parted with a small cucumber sandwich, too, so that Berryman would not starve. Two porters transferred the trunk from the hotel to a motor car, two more lifted it aboard the train, and it would doubtless take several additional men to carry it on board *Titanic*.

For all his annoying traits—his constant requests for money, his social insecurities, his illogically intense disdain for even the mildest stain—Berryman was essential. His knowledge of Bacon was profound, and his morals were delightfully malleable.

The train slowed as it passed through a small, poor town. Having no desire to witness depravity, Mr. Rockwell turned away. The woman beside him, thankfully, was sleeping. Hurriedly he devoured a small roast beef sandwich dripping with creamed horseradish. A dollop fell on the woman's dress, but he deftly scraped it up with a piece of paper so that only a small whitish stain remained.

Momentarily restored, he removed a brown folder from the case at his feet, pulled out a thin column of paper, and stared at it with delight: the alphabet of the Baconian cipher.

A   =   A A A A A

B   =   A A A A B

C   =   A A A B A

D   =   A A A B B

E   =   A A B A A

F   =   A A B A B

G   =   A A B B A

H   =   A A B B B

I-J   =   A B A A A

K   =   A B A A B

```
L = ABABA
M = ABABB
N = ABBAA
O = ABBAB
P = ABBBA
Q = ABBBB
R = BAAAA
S = BAAAB
T = BAABA
U-V = BAABB
W = BABAA
X = BABAB
Y = BABBA
Z = BABBB
```

He adored its simplicity, its subtle unpredictability. At the start, you'd naturally expect the position of that single B to keep moving left, but no, Bacon inserted an extra one when he arrived at the letter d, then reverted to the original pattern with e.

Using Bacon's alphabet, one could hide any message from the untrained eye. Sir Francis himself had used it to disguise the very treasure Rockwell sought—an equation of sorts. Of course it wouldn't be an equation in the standard modern sense, with symbolic notation and such. Mr. Rockwell liked to imagine that it would be a kind of written recipe.

He checked his recently wound gold watch and noticed with delight that he was only a few hours away from the volume. Widener would board *Titanic* at Cherbourg, France, and Berryman would procure the *Essaies* at the first opportunity.

Archibald Rockwell would not have to wait much longer.

TROUBLE IN BAGGAGE

For six days Patrick had done little but train. He learned how to polish silver, clean crystal, set tables, properly carry and stack china, replace linens, and more. He had his own uniform as well, though it was far too large in the collar. He could stick his whole hand through the gap between the shirt and his neck. Furthermore, Mr. Webb forced him to cut his hair, so his elephantine ears were now more prominent than ever.

The crew of stewards and waiters were thorough and relentless. They taught Patrick how to walk, stand, part and slick down his hair with pomade, and keep his shoes shining even after he'd trudged across the often wet galley floor. They also berated him. Constantly. Stand up straight! Fix your hair! Street urchin! That china is worth more than your life!

They swore they'd throw him into the sea if he left another

smudge on the silver. He was ordered to carry a spittoon with him all day, every day, and the men were all instructed to expectorate freely into the silver basin whenever they saw young Mr. Waters. Then, at the end of each day, he'd have to rinse the silver free of these black and yellow mouth juices, polish it to a mirror shine, and present it to Mr. Webb for inspection.

Though these were all grown men, they called him names, too: leprechaun, Paddy, dwarf, and more.

But he was learning. The criticisms became less frequent as one long day turned into the next, and any time he felt tired, or wondered whether it was really worth enduring all those insults and long, long days moistened by men's mucous, he thought of James and the Black Gang.

On one of their first nights aboard, James told him that a fire had begun in one of the bunkers. This wasn't unusual, James explained, but for some reason they weren't able to extinguish this one, and they were toiling harder than ever as a result. They had to put out the fire because they'd need to save as much coal as possible for the journey. They wanted it to burn in the boilers, not the storage bins.

Patrick stayed informed by hurrying down to the boiler rooms to see James whenever he could. The Black Gang continued to joke that he shouldn't linger for more than a few minutes, lest he faint again, but he felt comfortable there nonetheless, among his brother's friends. In fact, Patrick had hoped to continue sleeping in the trimmers' bunk room, to be closer to James, but Mr. Webb insisted that he move to the stewards' quarters. He probably wouldn't have seen much of his brother anyway, as James completely disregarded the schedule of four hours on and eight off. He worked until midnight and was up again at dawn.

By Wednesday morning they'd been docked in Southampton for seven days, and the first of the passengers were coming aboard. On his way up to the Smoking Room, Patrick passed Mr. Webb in the hall. Patrick held out a spittoon, which was already a quarter of the way full, and expected a formidable globule, but Mr. Webb declined.

"Walk with me if you would, Mr. Waters. The passengers have begun to board our great ship, so your job begins in earnest today."

"I'm ready, sir."

They walked in silence, descending several flights. Patrick failed to keep track of where they were, though he guessed that they had to be near the bow, and perhaps as low as G Deck.

"Might I ask where we're going, sir?"

As an answer Mr. Webb held up a handful of envelopes.

Two young crew members rushed past them on the stairs. "What is it boys?" Mr. Webb asked.

"Stowaway in baggage giving the men a bit of trouble," one yelled over his shoulder.

"A travesty!" Mr. Webb muttered. "*Titanic*'s maiden voyage should not be stained by ruffians. Now, you said that you were ready Mr. Waters, but that remains to be determined."

"Of course, sir, I only meant—"

"Quiet. You know, of course, that the Smoking Room is to be a haven for our privileged first-class gentlemen, a retreat where they can bask in sweet clouds of pipe smoke and enjoy the subtle burn of fine spirits as early or late as they like, shielded from the disapproving stares of their female companions, be they wives, mothers, or . . . friends. Colonel John Jacob Astor, one of the wealthiest men in the world, could very well be expectorating into one of your spittoons, Patrick."

They came to a landing with the door to baggage straight ahead and another, leading to the post office, on their right. The door to baggage swung open, and three men tumbled into the small hall, each flailing and kicking.

One of them, a decently dressed passenger, crawled backward out of the scrum unharmed. But the other two, crew members, were worse off: Blood streamed from the nose of one, and the other was pressing his fists to his eyes, yelling in pain.

Mr. Webb charged down the last few steps, then stopped, with his back to Patrick, and raised his hands. "There's no need to hurt anyone," he said.

Metal flashed in the light. The passenger—he had to be the

stowaway—was waving a knife with one hand and brushing the other over his suit, as if he were trying to smooth out its many wrinkles. "Stand back," he hissed.

Once Mr. Webb moved aside, Patrick saw the man clearly. He looked nothing like a ruffian. His suit and shirt were ruffled but not ragged. His face was unmarred by scars.

Holding out the long, bright knife, he moved past Webb, ordering the steward to his knees.

"Out of my way, boy!" he shouted at Patrick as he passed.

But Patrick couldn't simply let him by. Holding the spittoon by the rim, he hurled it like an axe. The silver vessel, turning end over end, hit the back of the man's head, and its vile contents washed out. A miniature waterfall of saliva poured over the back of the stowaway's suit jacket and down his neck.

The stowaway screamed and cursed, swiping and slapping at his neck as if he'd been set on fire. Turning, he glared at Patrick with eyes as red as the devil himself, then raced on up the stairs, disappearing into *Titanic*'s maze.

The crew member with the bloodied nose chased after him, but Mr. Webb calmly remained in place. "A noble effort, Mr. Waters," he said, "but I am disappointed."

"What?" Patrick asked. "Why?"

"You dropped your spittoon."

THE PRIZE OF THE HAY SALE

itanic steamed out of Southampton early Wednesday afternoon and stopped again off the coast of France. She was too large to approach the docks, so she waited offshore as large ferries called tenders carried out the next round of passengers.

Despite an intense search, no one had been able to find the stowaway. Patrick himself was not involved; the remainder of his day was a blur of people, a chorus of demands, and an endless procession of sullied plates, glasses, ashtrays, and spittoons. Men touring *Titanic* and seeing the Smoking Room for the first time entered with childlike joy, as if they'd come home. Numerous women declared it to be altogether too dark and unwelcoming, but one announced, "We need a room like this one."

A large older lady with frightfully red cheeks stared at Patrick skeptically as she passed through, but said nothing. A nice uniform, liberally applied pomade, proper posture, and he was passing for a seventeen-year-old!

By nine o'clock that evening, the end of his work day, Patrick was exhausted. He couldn't have been in his bed for more than a minute before he fell asleep. The next morning he rose early and caught James on his way out of the trimmers' bunks, but his brother had no time to talk. The fire in the storage bin was still burning.

Thursday proved to be slightly easier, but it passed in a rush nonetheless. Twelve hours felt like two, and as nine o'clock approached again, the Smoking Room was very nearly filled. Clouds of cigar smoke hung near the ceiling of the wood-paneled lounge. Electric lamps glowed yellow across the room, and voices boomed in conversation as mustached men in regal tuxedos reclined in leather sofas and chairs, smoking, chewing tobacco, playing cards. They sipped from fine crystal glasses brimming with inky wine and delicate, gold-rimmed porcelain cups harboring dark coffee.

Patrick was preparing to leave, setting clean ashtrays on the tables one last time, when Mr. Webb ordered the doors shut. Beside him stood a young man, perhaps a few years older than James, in a high-collared shirt and perfectly fitting tuxedo. His hair was slick, parted sharply down the middle, his back was straight, and his eyes were set in the shadows of large brows. He was no stranger to this class of men, yet his face bore a ghostly, panicked look. His large chin moved nervously from side to side.

The men ceased talking. Near the door to the galley Patrick saw a steward with thick, blond, tightly curled hair curse to himself.

"I deeply apologize, gentlemen," Mr. Webb began, "but one of your fellow passengers, Mr. Widener—"

"Harry Elkins Widener," the man added.

"Mr. Harry Elkins Widener has lost a book—"

"No, no, no! Not merely a book!" Mr. Widener interrupted. "A phenomenally old and rare book. The exquisite 1598 second edition of Sir Francis Bacon's *Essaies*, spelled with an *ie* instead of a *y*. Brown cover, some wear around the edges, but in good enough condition to be worth nearly as much as a new Renault."

An older passenger with gray hair, a gray mustache, and a well-fed stomach put his arm around him. "Harry, it will be found, you know."

"Thank you for your assurances, father, but I will sleep better when the prize of the Hay Sale is back in my possession."

The younger Widener again addressed the room. "I wouldn't dare imply that it was stolen, but perhaps one of you fine gentlemen mistakenly borrowed it? Or it might have fallen out of its case. I ask, please, search around you, and handle it carefully if you do find it, please. It is quite precious."

"Stewards and staff," Mr. Webb added, "please do as Mr. Widener asks."

Patrick had never heard anyone refer to a book that way. Precious? He could not resist smiling, and Widener caught him.

"You find this amusing?" he asked.

"No, I apologize, I—"

"This is an impossibly rare edition inscribed on the inside cover with a personal message from Sir Francis to his very own brother! I traveled here in part to procure this book, and I cannot lose it now."

"You steamed all the way to Europe for a book?"

Through clenched teeth Mr. Webb called to him. "Mr. Waters?"

"Yes?"

"The book, Mr. Waters. Quiet your tongue and put those sharp young eyes to work."

"Yes, of course, Mr. Webb." He nodded to Mr. Widener. "We'll find it, sir."

Across the room Patrick saw the blond steward pull his hand from behind one of the couches, then hurry off to another corner. Patrick walked to the couch, peering beneath several of the green leather chairs along the way, and saw a small brown pamphlet on the rug.

The title was clear enough in the light.

Patrick reached down to pick up the book, but Mr. Widener stopped him.

"No, no, allow me," he said. With delicacy he picked up the book, wrapped it in felt, and slipped it into a leather case. Then he patted the case and exhaled with relief. "Wonderful work, young man! Waters, is it? A handsome reward will be yours."

Patrick began to thank him, but Mr. Webb interrupted. "His only reward is your gratitude, Mr. Widener."

And with that, the Smoking Room returned to normal. The card games, momentarily disturbed, resumed. The stewards, finished with the pressure-filled treasure hunt, gladly took up their regular duties.

His book secure, Mr. Widener was now determined to hurry out of the lounge. As he crossed the room, Patrick noticed the odd blond steward standing beside an enormously round man smoking a massive pipe. They were both watching Harry Widener closely.

The steward caught Patrick's stare, rubbed the back of his neck, and turned away.

PLOTTING AMID POTATOES

He had the book! Only briefly, but he had it. The *Essaies* were safely and discreetly tucked away inside the annoying steward's jacket he had no choice but to wear. He could have easily slipped out of the Smoking Room. But then that spoiled prince Harry Widener noticed his precious possession was missing and erupted into a childish tantrum.

Painful as the act was, Berryman was forced to let go of the book they'd sought for so long; a glance from Mr. Rockwell assured him that this was the right decision. Their intentions could not be discovered so early in the voyage. If Widener knew there was a plot to steal the *Essaies*, he'd likely enlist an army to protect the book.

Once that young, spittoon-wielding pest "discovered" the lost book, Berryman left the room, descended to E Deck, and shut himself inside a large pantry packed with shelf after shelf of potatoes.

He couldn't help marveling at the spuds. He'd never seen so many potatoes before, and the earthy, brown, soil-rich smell was a shocking contrast to the tobacco laden air in the Smoking Room. He turned off the lights and welcomed the instant, comforting darkness. His eyes, head, and mind relaxed, and he sat on the cold floor, leaning against one of the shelves. He needed to think.

The time had come for a bold stroke. Given what they stood to gain, Berryman believed that any action which might draw them closer to their ultimate end was justifiable. Including murder. What would be so wrong with eliminating someone in the service of such an epic quest? Widener had already proven that he would be difficult. They needed no more obstacles, and with Widener gone they could study the book in peace.

It would give him so much pleasure to rid the world of Harry Elkins Widener. Berryman had not forgotten that slight in Harvard Yard; they had both arrived on campus for the very first time, and Harry saw him walking past. "Porter!" he called to him, holding up his bags. "Could you help with these?"

At the time, Berryman was young, nervous, and concerned that he did not belong among the rich and privileged boys. The mistake was devastating, yet he managed to politely inform Harry that he was, in fact, a student and not a porter. "Really?"

Harry responded as a group of first-years walked past, "but you so resemble a porter!" The others laughed, noticing Berryman's less than perfect clothes, and Harry walked onward in search of his lodgings.

For the rest of their time at Harvard, Harry was perfectly polite, even friendly. But Berryman never forgot that initial blow. Nor did the students who overheard it; he endured a number of porter jokes during his time at Harvard College. Harry effectively killed his chances of passing for a well-bred young man. Now, years later, the thought of killing Harry was rather alluring.

The act would be so, so easy aboard a massive ship like *Titanic*. Berryman was a skilled forger. He could draft a suicide note in Harry's hand, coax him into meeting late one night on an outside deck, then push him overboard and leave the note in his cabin. Simple!

He lifted a potato from the shelf behind him, turned it around in his hands. The plan was a perfect one, really. He would have to propose it to Mr. Rockwell.

MERELY A BOOK FOR BOYS

That night, following the incident in the Smoking Room, Patrick raced down to the boilers. Not only had he completed his first two days of work without any embarrassing accidents—he'd even been a success by some measures! He couldn't wait to tell James how he found the strange little book.

Two men he didn't know, their faces blackened with soot, passed him on the spiral stairs leading down to the boilers. "Is the fire out in number five?" he asked.

"She's blazing still," answered the larger of the two. "And I'd keep your mention of that fire to a minimum. We don't want the passengers worrying."

The heat intensified as he descended. His skin burned, as if he were pressing his face into an open oven. He saw Blaney first; his head was low and he was holding his hands as though he were bent in prayer. He moved like a man near death. "Martin? Is James still down there?"

Blaney lifted eyes as heavy as one of his iron shovels. "He is, and how I'll never know. Your brother is as strong as one of those turbines and as tireless. He won't rest until that fire is done."

Patrick hurried on, found James trimming with the energy of a man who'd just begun his very first shift. His shirt was tied around his head. His skin was burning red, covered with black soot and salted sweat. There was no point calling to him; his brother was in no state to be interrupted.

James stopped, wiped the sweat from his eyes with a cloth he'd tied around his wrist, and saw Patrick. James flicked the sweat-soaked rag at him. A corner of it caught his arm.

"Are you done already?" James asked. "You hardly look tired."

Patrick was embarrased to admit that Mr. Webb had dismissed him for the day. He didn't want James thinking he had a leisurely job. "No," he said, "only a break."

Minutes later, Patrick was back in the galley, standing before Mr. Webb. If he was going to honor the Waters name, he would have to work like his brother.

"I confess, I am impressed, Mr. Waters."

"Thank you, Mr. Webb."

"You've done a very adequate job, but for the rest of the evening I must put you in the service of an even more demanding customer than the first-class gentleman. I speak, of course, of the first-class lady. Our staff in the Reading & Writing Room is low at the moment and you would be useful there."

Patrick had no desire to spend more than a few minutes in that flowery refuge. "Thank you, Mr. Webb, but—"

"The Reading and Writing Room, Mr. Waters."

"Yes, sir."

Thankfully, the room was emptying when he arrived. A pair of white-haired women were quietly conversing over cups of tea. On the opposite side, near the large fireplace, another group was just standing to leave. A girl his age was with them; she was half-asleep and yawning dramatically.

At her side she held an enormous hat: a wide, white, heavily decorated creation with a circular brim. It was covered with flowers, ribbons, and bows. And were those birds? She was pretty, too, and she caught Patrick watching her. He silently cursed himself for staring too long and turned the opposite way. Only then did he notice the solitary figure sitting at a small table stacked with books.

The perfect tuxedo, the helmet of slicked hair, the posture, the books—it could only be Harry Widener. But what was he doing in a women's lounge? Patrick began to make his way to Widener's table for a closer look, but he was forced to stop as the group of women crossed the room.

For some reason he could not explain, Patrick bowed as they passed. The first woman stopped, the others did the same. She looked to be a few years younger than his own mother, and she smiled at Patrick with suspicion. "You are a steward?" she asked.

The silken, ribboned, made-up ladies before him were far more intimidating than the pipe-puffing men. He was too nervous to reply.

"You don't look a day over thirteen," the woman said. "About the same age as my Emily here."

Patrick tucked back his shoulders, flattened his hair and ears. Mr. Webb told him to lie, so he did. With confidence. "Seventeen in January, ma'am," he said firmly.

Satisfied, the woman nodded, and led her group onward.

Before they left, though, the girl, Emily, whispered back to him. "You're lying."

But Patrick had no chance to reply; Emily was gone, and Harry Widener began calling him.

"Mr. Waters! The steward who laughs at my passion."

Patrick hurried to his table. He replied humbly, "Sir, I apologize. I did not mean to offend you."

"What is your proper name?"

"Patrick. Patrick Waters."

"A good name. You'd have to live your life at sea with a surname like that, wouldn't you?"

Widener studied him and Patrick nervously tried to stand taller. Now, after that girl's comment, he felt young. He was not fit for inspection. He guessed that his uniform looked ridiculously large, his ears absurd.

"You are a junior steward, Patrick?" Widener asked skeptically.

"A very junior steward," he replied. The man was no fool; Patrick could see Widener knew that he was too young. "And yourself?"

"A book collector. Descended from a line of collectors, really. My grandfather collects paintings, my mother china and silver, and my uncle Joe collects a bit of everything. For the last few years I have been amassing a small but very respectable collection of rare volumes."

"A library," Patrick said, thinking of his father's old store of books.

"No, not a library. Though I do have three thousand books at this point, certainly enough to comprise a decent library."

Widener closed the book he was reading. Patrick spied the cover: *Treasure Island* by Robert Louis Stevenson. The story of pirates and buried gold was one of his father's favorites and, after his death, it was one of the first books his mother dispatched. Stevenson, according to his mother, was one of the primary reasons his father led the life he did. Stevenson so filled his head with adventures and dreams that there was no room for practical considerations, such as providing for one's family.

Thinking of his mother, Patrick regarded the book with disdain.

"You don't approve? Astonishing!" Widener said. "A seagoing lad such as yourself—this should be your Bible! What do you have against this book?"

"Nothing, sir."

"Harry. Please, please, please call me Harry, and do not lie to me, either. I saw the look on your face. It was as if you'd been asked to chew on a wool sock. None of my associates in books or in business understand my devotion to this author, either. Their opinions I can comprehend, to some degree. But why a boy of your age should have something against Stevenson I simply cannot fathom. Please, enlighten me, Patrick."

None of the other stewards were in the room, so whatever he said would not get back to Mr. Webb. "My honest answer?"

"Your honest answer."

Patrick summoned his mother's own words. "Stevenson is a distraction, and that book is filled with wild dreams and fantasies that serve no purpose but to keep boys and men from taking seriously their real duties in the world."

Outraged, Harry covered the book with his arms, as if to prevent the novel, or even Stevenson himself, from hearing such blasphemy.

Patrick continued: "Stevenson isn't the only villain. All novels and, indeed, all but a few books in all the libraries of the world are entertainments that keep man from his true calling. A man should toil on his feet, not read in a chair."

Harry's already pale face lost still more color. His dark eyes sank farther beneath the cover of his large brow. "My, God, boy! Who has poisoned you?"

A PROPENSITY FOR TOIL

At dawn the next morning Patrick dropped to the floor from the upper bunk. A shock spread through his feet. His legs were aching; even his back was sore. The previous day had to have been the longest he'd ever spent standing.

The pain reminded him of what he'd said to Harry Widener the evening before. A man should toil on his feet? Is that what he'd said? Reading in a chair was far more appealing to Patrick now.

Widener had reacted so strangely to his comment. Patrick had gone on to tell him about his father, the books, and how he'd been out of school for over a year. Harry appeared to listen closely, but he said nothing. Then, finally, he announced that he had to turn in for the night. He thanked Patrick, collected his books, and left the room.

Now Patrick stared at his two matching uniforms hanging on the edge of the bed. Careful not to wake the snoring stewards all around him, he chose one and quietly shook it a few times, as if this might wake it up. Then he slipped on the pants, shirt and coat, and headed for the trimmers' bunks. It was early enough; there was a chance he'd see James.

The trimmers and firemen were intentionally separated from the rest of the boat. Their bunks, mess halls, and washrooms were hard to access, but Patrick's regular treks through *Titanic's* tangle of passageways and stairs had made him a kind of expert on the boat's interior. You often had to go up to get down or walk astern to access a room near the bow. He had a feel for it all now.

A layer of coal dust settled on his tongue the moment he entered the trimmers' bunks; the men exhaled the stuff as they snored. His brother's bed was empty again, the mattress and blanket undisturbed. Blaney was not there, either.

Patrick's eyes were still clouded with sleep, so he opened a faucet at the nearest washbasin. Frigid seawater poured out. Patrick splashed some on his face, the back of his neck, and ran a handful through his hair. The water was salty and fresh; he rinsed and spat, clearing out the dust. Had he offended Widener somehow?

"Evening, Patrick," Blaney grumbled behind him.

"It's morning, Martin."

Eyes closed, dressed in his sweat-soaked clothes, Blaney collapsed on his bunk. "And how would I know that?"

"Is James coming?" Patrick asked, but he received no reply. Blaney was already asleep.

Down in the bunkers, Patrick absorbed the rhythmic thumping of the engines, the hiss of the burning coal, the forced breathing of the exhausted men, and watched his brother shoveling and stoking from afar. James was as much a part of *Titanic* now as one of her engines.

The chief engineer, Joseph Bell, stopped Patrick on his way out. "Look at yourself! A fainting trimmer last week, a proper steward now."

There was mockery in his voice, but Patrick ignored it. "The fire," he responded, "it's still going?"

"It is, but we're making headway, and the result of it won't be all bad. Shoveling all this coal into the boilers helps us run faster. There's been talk of breaking the record for an Atlantic crossing. Now," he said, "off to your spittoons before you collapse."

Up on A Deck, the main rooms and halls were nearly deserted. Patrick walked out to the first-class promenade. One of the sliding glass windows was open slightly and he pressed his face through. Cold air swept across his skin, ran over his hardened hair. He breathed deeply and let the sea breeze rush through him.

The water was gray and perfectly calm, an aquatic desert

without a single dune. They were surrounded by the sea, heading west across the Atlantic. Two weeks earlier he could not have imagined he would be in such a position. Patrick Waters, at sea! Really, truly at sea, without a speck of land for hundreds, even thousands of miles. The scene was overwhelming, intimidating. Once or twice before in his life he had felt something similar in church, but nothing quite like this, nothing quite so expansive. The sea made him feel like he was part of something far, far grander than himself.

"Mr. Waters! Would you like a cup of warm chocolate while you're enjoying the view?"

"I was just—"

"As long as you are on *Titanic* you are on the job," Mr. Webb said. He reached out and adjusted Patrick's tie, then brushed his hand across his shoulder. "Down in the engine rooms, were you? The passengers won't tolerate coal-covered stewards, Mr. Waters. If you must visit your brother, leave your jacket at your bunk."

Patrick glanced at his other shoulder, swept off a fine layer of dust.

"Your appearance is doubly important today, Mr. Waters, because as of this morning, you have a new position."

"Sir, they asked me how old I was, so I—"

"How old? What are you talking about, Mr. Waters? I'm trying to tell you that for some unknowable reason, Mr. Harry Widener has requested that you be reassigned. He has asked that you serve as his personal steward. Although I still require your labor, however simple and unskilled it may be, I cannot deny a man of Mr. Widener's wealth and stature. You begin this morning."

Patrick should not have spoken so honestly the night before. Undoubtedly Harry planned to punish him. "What will I be asked to do?"

"Fetch, I imagine," he said. "Fresh cigars, coffee, a coat if he wishes to walk outside."

He had no desire to be a dog. Clearly this was Widener's way of exacting revenge for what Patrick had said about books. Yet Patrick couldn't explain that to Mr. Webb. "Sir, I understand that Mr. Widener is a powerful man, but I'm only just growing accustomed to my role, thanks to your attentive training," Patrick said, "and I would really rather not give that up, while I am still learning." Mr. Webb was listening, but appeared to be unmoved. "The spittoons, sir," Patrick added, "I'm hardly a demigod yet."

"Have no fear of that, Mr. Waters. You have shown a propensity for toil, so you will work for Mr. Widener when he demands it, which will only amount to a portion of the day. For the rest of your waking hours, you will work for me." Mr. Webb winked. "I would not dare separate you from your precious saliva."

HARRY WIDENER'S SCHOOL
FOR ILL-INFORMED STEWARDS

Beside a tall window in the Reading & Writing Room,
Harry Widener sat straight-backed with three books on
the table before him. A few passengers were enjoying tea. There
were several stewards on hand: an Englishman named Cheverton, Moore, and a man with slick black hair, a large and impres-
sively spiraling mustache, a prodigious belly, and incongruously
thin arms and legs. By that point Patrick knew or at least recognized most of the staff, as they'd all taken the time either to in-
sult him or to expectorate into one of his spittoons. But this man,
who was carefully dusting a mantle near Harry, had never called
him a name or spat his way.

After several slow breaths Patrick steeled himself for Harry's
revenge. "Good morning, sir," he said as he approached. His mouth
was dust dry. "May I bring you something?"

"No, no, and good morning to you, Patrick. You've heard of my request then? Good. Well, I should tell you forthwith that yours will not be a normal steward's position."

Patrick looked down at the intricately patterned rug. "If you are upset about what I said last night, sir, regarding *Treasure Island*, I apologize if I offended you, but you did ask for my opinion."

The steward of strange proportions knocked over a small clock on the mantle. He quickly righted his mistake.

"First, I remind you again that my name is Harry. My father is Mr. Widener. Second, I am delighted you proffered your opinion. My concern, though, is that I suspect it isn't entirely your opinion. When I was your age, all of my so-called opinions were borrowed from my elders. My mother, mostly. Only through books and learning and, of course, deep thinking, did I begin to develop and cultivate my own ideas." He lovingly patted the books on the table. "Given that you have professed such intolerance for these printed pamphlets of human wisdom and frailty, I worry that you will never have such an opportunity, Patrick, and that you will proceed through life brandishing the ideas of others as your own. This is the way of the masses, but it is no way to live." Harry pushed back his chair, stood up, and placed both hands on Patrick's shoulders. "Your new role, therefore, will not be so much steward as student."

"Student?" Patrick sank. He did not sneak aboard the ship to return to school. "But sir . . . Harry, I'm a working man now."

"Yes, and I've arranged it so that, at least for the duration of this voyage, your primary occupation will be to listen and learn."

Neither James nor Blaney would approve. His mother would be supremely disappointed. "That isn't work!" he protested.

The disproportioned waiter had moved closer; he was now wiping the table next to them with a damp yellow rag.

Harry waved to the man. "Excuse me? Would you like to join us, is that it?"

"My apologies, Mr. Widener."

"Please leave us alone, Mr . . ."

The steward failed to respond.

"You do know your name, don't you?"

"S-sorry, sir. Yes. The name is Coleman, and I'll do as you wish."

The steward exited as ordered.

"I can think of few things less tolerable than eavesdropping servants. Now, what was it you said, Patrick?"

"I said that reading isn't work. Reading is leisure."

Harry's large eyes grew wider as he held up the book he'd lost the day before. "Reading a book like this is the hardest work a man could ever do, Patrick! Understanding its place in the history of human thought? That is as noble and challenging an endeavor as any."

Gently Harry put the book back on the table. Patrick reached down to pick it up, but Harry stopped him. "No, no, Patrick, we won't be reading *that* copy."

"Why not?"

"Because it is rare. One of only four extant copies—"

Patrick's face betrayed his ignorance, and Harry stopped. "Extant?" Patrick asked.

"*Remaining*," Harry explained. "Only four early copies of Bacon's *Essaies* remain in the world, and this is one of the finest, inscribed with a loving note to his brother, Anthony. Reading it is strictly out of the question. A stain, an accidental rip, any such mishap could drastically reduce its value."

A small chuckle escaped Patrick. He could not help himself: Harry's logic was ridiculous. After being lectured on the wisdom contained in that book, Patrick was told that he was not actually allowed to read it. How could he not laugh?

"I have a replica for you to peruse instead," Harry said. "It is a near exact facsimile reproduction printed not long ago, in 1904. What is it? Why are you smiling?"

"Sir, Harry, I don't understand. Why is that one so important if there are exact reproductions with the same words, the same knowledge, even the same design?"

"Because the original is a symbol of this great man's interaction with the world at large! An early edition is representative of his urgent need to impress these ideas upon mankind. These reproductions . . . they are meaningless as objects. But this, this 1598 edition, it is a critical object, arguably as important to the history of human knowledge as Michelangelo's *David* is to the history of human art. Wait . . . you do know of the *David*, don't you?"

Patrick gazed blankly at the clock on the mantle. His father had taught him countless strange facts, but they never covered art.

"Amazing. Why they let boys into the world without such knowledge is utterly incomprehensible. The *David* is widely recognized as the world's greatest sculpture. Michelangelo, its creator, is one of the true giants of the Renaissance. This man," he said, holding up the *Essaies*, "is the Michelangelo of human wisdom."

"So how valuable is it?"

"How valuable? I've just told you, Patrick."

The group from the previous night, including the girl, strode through and took the couch and chairs beside the fireplace. Emily held the same hat at her side; now Patrick was certain there were birds among all those multicolored flowers and ribbons and lace; a number of them, in fact.

He tried to ignore the group and the girl. There were other stewards. His job now was to serve Harry.

"I meant how valuable in terms of money?" Patrick pressed.

Carefully Harry turned the book over, glanced over the cover and the edges. "More than a modest home, I should say."

"That!" he said, pointing at the slim, heavily aged, glorified pamphlet. "That book is worth more than a home?"

"Well, not my home, of course," Harry continued. "Lynnewood Hall has over one hundred five rooms. But the average home? Yes, I should say this book is worth more. Far more, in my estimation."

The book was dark and frail and brittle, merely a collection of old paper.

"I don't understand," Patrick said at last.

"Yes, well, some do understand its value, and I suppose that's why I was in such a state last night. My imagination took hold for a moment and I thought someone might be trying to steal the book. Hence my request that Mr. Webb close the doors."

Patrick recalled the odd blond steward and the man with the pipe. They had both been watching Harry closely. He said nothing, but Harry could see him thinking.

"What is it Patrick?" Harry leaned forward, excited, and spoke in a conspiratorial whisper. "Please sit and tell me, Patrick. Did you see someone try to steal my book last night?"

For a moment Patrick considered saying nothing, but Harry begged for more details. Finally he yielded, settled into the cushioned chair, and told Harry what he thought he'd seen.

"Curly blond hair, you say? We'll have to watch out for him," he whispered. "But if he is a thief, he certainly is an unusual one. There are far more valuable items on board this ship; my mother's jewels, for instance. Those alone could buy an entire neighborhood of respectable homes. So we should consider the possibility that he wants this volume for reasons other than its market value. There is the chance—"

"The chance of what?"

"No, no, Patrick. My boyish imagination sometimes breaks the shackles of my better judgment."

Patrick could think of no reasonable way to convince him to go on. So he clasped his hands eagerly before him and asked, "Please?"

"I suppose it might . . . and I very much mean *might* . . . contain a hidden message."

Harry glanced over his shoulder at the table of women. Emily was watching them—now she was the one who turned away, her cheeks aflame.

"You see, Patrick, Sir Francis Bacon was a developer of ciphers and a member of several powerful secret societies. I suppose it's possible—*merely possible*—that the book harbors a secret message of some sort."

"What kind of message?" he asked.

Harry waved his hands before his face, as if he were physically swatting the topic out of the air. "No, no, enough of that. We are here to learn, not engage in rumors."

This was too enticing; Patrick couldn't just move on. He

picked up the reproduction, thumbed through, then leaned forward. "If I promise to read the first twenty pages, will you tell me more?"

"It's better not to think of read pages as progress. The book is broken into statements. There are one hundred two in total. You are to read . . . one."

He had expected ten, maybe twenty. One would be easy. "Fine. Now, what about the messages?"

Harry gently wrapped the second edition in the green felt, folded it over, and slipped the book into the dark brown leather case. Then he took the other three books and placed them under his arm. "If we are to wrap ourselves in the mysteries of Sir Francis Bacon, I will require a second cup of coffee. Hot. Procure that, find yourself a suitable coat, and meet me on the promenade."

STATESMAN, SCIENTIST, SWINDLER

After they had strolled quietly for some time along the glass-enclosed promenade, past lounging passengers and doting stewards, Harry finished his coffee, handed Patrick the cup, and declared that he wanted to truly feel the sea air, to directly breathe in the cold fresh breeze. The Boat Deck would be the place, he said, and so they marched up. Patrick held on to the empty cup; he could find nowhere to deposit it. Up top, Harry waved Patrick over to a railing near one of the lifeboats on the port side and, for a few moments, they merely watched.

The sea was a bright, shining gray, almost the tint of a partially polished spittoon. All around the boat the water was flat, unmarred by ripples. Behind them, *Titanic*'s wake spread out toward the horizon, her waves white and frothy at first, then smooth in the distance.

Patrick had never enjoyed such an uninterrupted, uncrowded view. He had lived all his life in a city, surrounded by tightly packed blocks of buildings. All he ever saw was brick and stone. Out here was all vast, empty space. He felt as if he were standing atop a mountain and gazing out at the very edge of the world. He had a strange, strong urge to soar off into the distance like some giant, wide-winged bird.

"It is a strange thing," Harry began, "that in sea voyages, where there is nothing to be seen, but sky and sea, men should make diaries; but in land travel, wherein so much is to be observed, for the most part they omit it; as if chance were fitter to be registered than observation."

If Harry expected him to understand any of that, he had severely overestimated Patrick's intelligence. "Excuse me?"

"A line from Bacon's entry on travel," Harry explained. "I thought it fitting, given this scene. Bacon was not complimenting the sea so much as criticizing man, yet I believe there is an important point within that statement. The sea in all her infinite sameness does make one think."

"So Bacon was a traveler."

"And more! A philosopher, statesman, scientist, and a bit of a swindler."

"Those don't quite piece together."

"Maybe *swindler* is the wrong word," Harry said. "Let's call him an amoral opportunist. He prosecuted his own uncle to gain favor with the Queen, then published a pamphlet apologizing when the political winds shifted."

"I imagine his uncle didn't forgive him," Patrick said.

"He did not have the chance! He had already been executed, in part because of Bacon's indictment. And I doubt Bacon was truly repentant. He probably only published the pamphlet because the new ruler, King James I, was sympathetic to his uncle's ideals."

"He doesn't sound particularly gracious."

"No, but the mind of the man, the ideas!" Harry said. "You know his famous statement, of course."

Embarrassed, Patrick looked away.

"*Knowledge is power*! Everything he did and thought is contained in that simple statement. And he accomplished quite a great deal. He developed the precursor to what we know as the scientific method, the idea that we must proceed from facts and not prejudices. He wrote tracts on philosophy and government and morals. He developed ciphers that many believe to have been influential in the development of secret societies, of which he was also known to be a member. He was imprisoned for his debts, for corruption, and some even believe him to be the true author of the plays attributed to William Shakespeare. And you might appreciate this," Harry said, his eyes opening wide, "he entered college at the age of twelve."

Executions, codes, secret societies, college at twelve! The man truly must have been a genius.

"If the story is to be believed, he also died a glorious death. Not by sword, but in the quest to conquer nature."

Harry motioned to a bench behind them, at the base of one of the great, towering, soot-spewing funnels, and they each sat. Looking west, he guessed. On the far end of the adjacent bench, the balloon-shaped passenger from the Smoking Room was reclining with his eyes closed and his full face aimed toward the dull and distant sun, sleeping. Patrick hadn't noticed him until they'd turned to sit; he'd tell Harry about the man later, in private.

Patrick had not yet found a place to deposit the cup, and his hands had grown cold from holding it in the damp ocean air. He placed it on the deck beneath the bench, warned himself not to forget, and shoved his hands deep into his pockets.

"So, Sir Francis Bacon," Harry resumed. "Did I mention he was knighted? Yes? Well, Sir Francis was traveling from London to an estate in Highgate one evening when he was struck with an idea. It had been snowing heavily and Bacon thought the cold snow might offer a way to preserve meat. Remember, there were no ice chests then. So, he immediately sought a nearby farm and, in the dead of night, purchased two slaughtered chickens from a farmer. He then proceeded to stuff the insides of these fowl full of snow and surround the snow-stuffed meat with still more snow so that it was all completely entombed in ice, inside and out."

"Did it work?"

"I don't know," Harry answered. "But not more than three days later he died of pneumonia."

The story reminded him of something his father might've tried. Something his mother would mock unmercifully. "That doesn't sound brilliant or noble. He sounds like a fool."

"This was all in the passionate pursuit of knowledge!"

"But he died."

"Yes, yes, he died, but it's the spirit you should consider here, Patrick, not the outcome. The zeal that kept him out in that bone chilling cold. The same spirit that drove him to his great accomplishments: the philosophical works, the scientific method, these essays!" Harry said, holding up the leather case. "Even the Shakespeare—it would not surprise me if he were the real Shakespeare."

A heavy hand clamped down on Patrick's shoulder, and Harry's face flushed red.

"If he had the same passion for railroads, we would be bigger than Morgan." Gray, distinguished, and smelling of pipe smoke, Harry's father moved his hand to his son's shoulder. His wide waistline and happy smile suggested that this was not a man who had to struggle to enjoy life.

"Ready for lunch, Harry?" he asked.

Patrick's tutor stammered, shook his head. Harry's energy disappeared; he slouched at his father's appearance as if he'd been caught doing something illegal.

"Yes, father, of course," Harry answered. He moved the case behind his back, apparently embarrassed by his books. "This is Patrick Waters."

"A lift boy?"

"No, a steward. Right, Patrick?"

"That is the official position, yes sir, but Harry has turned me into his student."

"Be careful not to take in too much, Patrick. My son here has more knowledge packed behind that forehead of his than any practical man could ever use."

He said this with a smile, and the shadow of a laugh, but Harry clearly didn't enjoy the joke. Without a word, or even a note of protest, he pointed his polished black loafers in another direction, pressed his precious book to his chest, and walked away.

Patrick expected Harry's father to be angry; men of their class were not accustomed to such treatment. But George Widener said nothing. He unleashed a great sigh and, with heavy steps, he followed him.

Not knowing what to say or do, or even whether he should say or do anything at all, Patrick remained quietly in his spot, the soles of his shoes effectively nailed to the newly stained wooden deck. Only when Mr. Widener was out of view did Patrick start to move.

He remembered the cup after two steps. As he reached back to retrieve it, an unfamiliar voice called to him.

"Come here, boy! I have a question for you."

The balloon-shaped man was sitting up, beckoning.

"Yes, sir?" he said, cup in hand.

"Tell me, boy, what would you say to earning two years' wages for a few hours' work?"

SIR ROBIN'S PROPOSAL

With tremendous effort the man rose to his feet, exhaling in great gusty bursts. Balance did not come quickly. There was a dazed and dizzy look to him for a moment or two, and a slight sway. Only then, watching him struggle and sway, did Patrick notice the man's very small feet. "Italian," the man said, steadying himself at the rail. "Florentine, to be precise. The only place in the world to find truly artisanal shoes."

"Oh, yes," Patrick replied, thankful he had mistaken his stare, "they are . . . marvelous."

"Archibald Rockwell is the name."

Patrick extended his hand, readied it for a firm grip.

"I do not shake hands, young man."

"My apologies," Patrick said. He joined his hands behind his back. "I'm Patrick Waters."

"Yes, I know, I've discovered that."

"Can I offer you something, sir? A cup of warm chocolate, perhaps?"

"Hmmmm . . . I'm not one to turn down the offer of food or drink, but this once I'll say no, Patrick. Of course, you don't mind if I call you Patrick? I can't permit you to call me Archibald, naturally. Mr. Rockwell will do. But do not let that formality befuddle you; we shall become very close before long, I believe. Put out your hand."

Mr. Rockwell promptly dropped a shilling into his palm. The coin was nothing to scoff at, but it was hardly two years' pay. At Patrick's wage of three pounds per month, that would be nearly seventy-five pounds! The shilling was a pittance in comparison.

"Sir, this is not necessary—"

"Quiet, Patrick," he snapped. "Hold out your other hand." Now Rockwell gave him a small iron nail. "Tell me which is worth more."

This had to be some sort of trick question, but he couldn't see the trick. Patrick did know that one could buy an entire box of nails for roughly that amount; only a month earlier, after a few unruly patrons had done some damage to the bar, Mr. Joyce had sent him on an errand to buy materials for the repairs. "The shilling," he said.

"In the world that most humans see and understand, you would be perfectly correct. But I am on the cusp of entering another world, one in which the value of metals lies not in their present state, as a key or a coin, but in what they can become."

Mr. Rockwell dug through one of his pockets for what Patrick guessed would be another shilling, but produced a small sandwich instead. Sliced turkey, from what Patrick could see. He eyed it with disappointment, placed it back in his pocket, and resumed his lecture.

"Did Mr. Widener mention that Sir Francis Bacon was an alchemist? Oh, don't look so astounded, young man. This corpulent shell might be soft, but my mind and ears are sharp. I am very interested in that little volume Mr. Widener carries around."

"I saw you with that steward. Were you trying to steal it?"

"It's dangerous to accuse a passenger of theft, Patrick."

"But I saw you both—"

"You saw what, precisely? Two men talking? Are you familiar with the tale of Sir Robin, Patrick?"

He shook his head.

"Perhaps you'd know him by another name: Robin Hood. The ruling authority of his day considered Sir Robin a thief, but the people thought him a hero, because he stole from the rich and gave to the poor."

"I'm no crook," Patrick said. He bowed slightly and started to walk away.

Mr. Rockwell's fingers closed around Patrick's arm; it felt as if he'd been grabbed by a number of very small pillows. "Wait, please. It is in your best interest to listen to my proposal, Patrick."

He reached into his coat for what Patrick feared would be a pistol or knife, then removed a cold chicken drumstick wrapped in a dinner napkin. Between eager bites he urged Patrick back to the rail.

"That little book of Mr. Widener's contains a very vital scrap of information. I merely wish to extract this scrap, after which I will happily return the book to Mr. Widener."

"Why not ask him to borrow it?"

"Ha! You are no simpleton, are you, Patrick? This information could grant tremendous power and wealth. Your Harry is already an immensely wealthy man. He has no need for more, and he would likely use any excess funds to buy more books and fineries. Trifles! I, on the other hand, will redistribute this wealth, like our friend Sir Robin. And you, Patrick, would be the first beneficiary of my generosity. What are the monthly wages of a steward, Patrick? Four pounds?"

"Three pounds and fifteen shillings for most, sir. But I'm down at three even on account of my age."

"A travesty!" Mr. Rockwell declared. "Now you see, Patrick, I could have offered you a pound or two. Most men would grasp the chance to earn a week's pay in an hour. But I am a generous man, Patrick. I am no wealthy miser, no hoarder of paintings

and rare books like the Wideners. So I offer you the very gracious sum of fifty pounds for your services."

A blast of cold sea air chilled him through. Though it wasn't
the two years' wages he'd promised at first, fifty pounds was
an incredible sum. His mother would be thrilled if he brought
home half that much. But he could not steal. "You are a worker,
Patrick, not a wealthy intellectual layabout like Harry Elkins
Widener. A worker! I can see that. And I can see that you are
suspicious. Rightly so, as men of my generous nature are a rarity
in this world. But consider it this way: All I am offering you is a
more lucrative working arrangement. In lieu of your normal,
meager pay, you will receive a hefty sum."

"I . . ." Patrick stammered, unable to bring himself to decline.
He was no longer certain his morals should apply. Maybe it would
not be so wrong, if so much good could come of the act.

"Quiet, young man, quiet," Mr. Rockwell said, directing Patrick astern. "I do not require an answer immediately. What I
would like is for you to secure the book for me on occasion, so
that I might study it in brief stints during the duration of our
voyage. The events in the Smoking Room have made it evident
that if Mr. Widener's book were outright stolen, he would stop
this very ship until it was found."

"That's why you returned it."

"I admit to nothing, but that would be the logical response,"
he said, nibbling the last bits of fat, peppered skin, and oily

cartilage from the chicken bone. Then he tossed the stripped bone over a wall. "Oh don't look so mortified, Patrick! I threw it at those beasts in second class."

Next Mr. Rockwell reached out and wiped the last traces of chicken fat on Patrick's lapel.

"I will be in my cabin, B-79, tomorrow, Sunday, before lunch," he said. "You can bring me the book then and there."

UNLIKELY BURGLAR

Titanic had already traveled eight hundred miles by lunch on Saturday. The men in the engine room said the massive blades were pushing her through the flat, frigid Atlantic at near record speeds. The air continued to cool; passengers now wore heavy coats when taking the air on deck, and the stewards complained about the increased calls for cups of warm chocolate and hot bouillon.

For lunch that afternoon, first-class passengers enjoyed a rich and fattening feast, including roasted squab slathered with currant jam, curried lamb chops, cheese-smothered potatoes, and salty, searing hot onion soup.

At each meal the amount of food served was staggering, far too much for all but the most gluttonous passengers. Plates upon plates of partially eaten meals—a mere spoonful of mashed potatoes removed from a mountainous mound—came back into the kitchen. Teams of dishwashers would scrape cheese-slathered vegetables, sauce-soaked meats, bones, and berries down metal chutes that led straight to the sea. Patrick heard the dishwashers wonder aloud whether the fish lucky enough to swim across the remains of these expertly prepared meals would enjoy them more or less than the passengers. Could sharks develop a liking for lamb?

Seated at a table of accomplished men, Harry was barely enduring the long lunch, frequently tapping the leather case that contained the *Essaies*. While his father and his friends conversed with enthusiasm and cheer, Harry looked as though he would rather be in his cabin, reading.

Across the room, Mr. Rockwell happily feasted. As a waiter removed Mr. Rockwell's third consecutive cleared plate, Patrick Waters watched him through a mildly foggy porthole in one of the swinging galley doors.

A waiter bearing two trays in one arm cursed at Patrick in what sounded like French.

"Excuse me," Patrick said, grabbing his free arm, "how many courses?"

"*Huite!*" the waiter replied.

A second waiter followed behind him, adding, "That means eight."

Which meant Patrick had ample time. Four more courses

remained, and he doubted that Mr. Rockwell would refuse a single one.

He wasn't due to meet Harry again until three o'clock, and he had managed to avoid Mr. Webb, who would undoubtedly assign him to a room if he found out that Patrick was free. There was no studying for him to do—Harry had mentioned a reading assignment, but he'd forgotten to give him the book. This was a lucky oversight, as he had a more pressing concern. He had to find out more about Mr. Rockwell.

Unfortunately there was no simple way to do so. Asking the other passengers was out of the question, and the stewards would hardly be forthcoming, either: They'd remind him that he was not supposed to wonder about the passengers. He was merely supposed to serve them. Yet he had to know if this was a man he could trust. Simply accepting the proposal would be too risky. What if Mr. Rockwell were caught? What if he blamed it all on Patrick? They'd listen to a passenger, not a junior steward.

At the same time, he was in no position to reject the proposal outright. That would be unthinkable, given the sum. The only course of action was to perform some direct research of his own. He would inspect Mr. Rockwell's cabin while the man was dining.

Luckily he did not encounter Mr. Webb in the halls or on the stairs, and he reached the first-class cabins on B Deck without so much as a nod from any other members of the crew. Normally this was not his place; he was supposed to confine himself to the crew alleyways and his assigned rooms. In fact, he realized that it had been a week since he'd seen the clean white halls or stepped on the soft red rugs that lined them. A week since he'd talked his way aboard. He felt the loose but stiff collar against his neck, glanced down at his polished black shoes. His mother would surely glow at the sight of him now.

"What are you doing?"

That girl with the hat. Emily. She had caught him standing there appreciating himself. "Me? Nothing," he stammered. "No-where?"

"Nowhere?"

"I meant to say that I'm not going anywhere," Patrick replied.

Ever so slightly she smirked. His face was hot and his collar now felt like a piece of sandpaper against his neck.

"Emily," she said.

"I know. I'm Patrick."

Would they shake hands? He readied his, but Emily raised her thin fingers to the brim of her large, bird-adorned hat, tipped it slightly, and continued past him down the hall. Once she was gone, Patrick rushed forward to the door with the etched marble oval reading B-79. He tried the handle.

What a fool! Of course it was locked. What had he been thinking? Mr. Rockwell would not simply leave his door open for anyone to enter.

"I can help, if you like."

Emily was walking back his way, hat in hand.

"What are you doing?" he asked.

She pointed to the carpet behind him, where a small key lay on the floor. "I dropped it," she said.

Patrick picked up the key and handed it to her, hoping she'd be on her way. Instead, she stared at the lock.

"Let me guess, one of the men forgot his precious pipe?"

Patrick did not have to lie, as she resumed before he could reply. "Practically the entire ship is outfitted with these," she said, kneeling at the edge of the door to inspect the lock. "May I?"

His expression answered for him, and Emily removed a pair of pins from her complicated hat.

The hat was distracting. "Are those . . . hummingbirds?"

"Why yes they are! There's a finch here, too, hiding in the back between a pair of matching bows. I wanted a blue jay as well, for the color mostly, but they are far too large."

Patrick could not think of how to respond. It was certainly the oddest piece of headwear he'd ever seen. "It's . . ."

"I call it my aviary," she said. Then she inserted the pins, one atop the other, and proceeded with deep concentration to oper-ate on the lock.

"They are made by the Smadbeck Lock Company which, as anyone with any sense knows, produces completely inadequate products. Harland and Wolff spared almost no expense in building *Titanic*, but on locks, they went cheap."

"How do you know all that?" Patrick said.

Without looking up Emily replied, "My family is in the lock business, but Harland and Wolff deemed our products too expensive. Father is still smoldering over the decision, so he refused to come home with us on *Titanic*, but Mother wanted the experience." The lock clicked, a smile brightened her face, and Emily pushed down on the handle. "But we don't keep valuables in our room!"

Emily stepped through. "Are you coming in?"

THE MANY FACES OF MR. ROCKWELL

Mr. Rockwell's small cabin appeared to have been violently shaken. Clothes were thrown about and piled in the corners. Several valises lay open on the floor—shirts and pants were dangling over the edges. Small, elegant leather shoes of varying colors and shades were spread about, laying on the pillows, hanging by their laces from the wardrobe and the dressing table.

The bed was a disheveled disaster and the room reeked of old Stilton and unintentionally aged broccoli. Which was no great wonder, really, given that there were plates of food scattered everywhere. Some were half-cleared, others entirely full, as if they'd come straight from the kitchen.

The sole signs of order in the entire cabin were a neatly laid out blanket and pillow on the sofa and, on the dressing table, neat stacks of papers and a number of old, leather books with thick, rough-edged pages. Patrick studied the titles, but most were in languages he could not read. There were strange symbols instead of the usual letters. Only one—*The New Physics*—was in English.

Emily eyed the leather spines. "Arabic."

"He reads Arabic?"

"Who?" she asked impatiently. "Tell me, Patrick, why have I allowed you in here? If the galley is missing some china, I believe you've found the culprit."

Patrick picked up one of the books. "Can you read it?"

"I can't read the language, only recognize it. We spent several months in Baghdad when I was ten. But listen, Patrick, I don't understand what we're doing here. I haven't assisted a petty thief, have I?"

"No, of course not! I . . ."

She moved toward the door. "I shouldn't have helped you . . . I'll have to tell someone."

"No, wait, please," he said. "Let me explain."

"Be honest with me."

There was not a hint of deceit in her eyes. "Can I trust you?" he asked.

"Of course."

In a rush he told her everything.

Emily needed no time to reflect. She huffed like an old woman. "That certainly sounds like theft."

"But not if we return it! If Harry doesn't know it's gone, and the book isn't damaged, then no one will be wronged! How could that be theft?"

"You've made your decision then."

"No, no, that's why I'm here. I need to find out more about this man."

"What does he have to do with it? Your decision should be clear regardless of his character. Besides, I could have told you about him. My mother knows him," she said casually. "When she first saw him in the dining saloon she referred to him as a . . . oh, what was it? Yes: a buffoonish braggart. I guess he's quite full of himself. That said, she did not say anything suggesting that he might be a criminal."

A buffoon Patrick could deal with, if it meant fifty pounds.

"I could find out more if you like."

Patrick heard something outside the door. Footsteps, perhaps. Then the sound was gone.

"Yes, that would be an enormous help."

"Then let's go."

He agreed with a nod, but could not resist another glance at the materials on Rockwell's desk. Below the book he'd picked up lay a single strip of thick, dimpled paper. Short combinations of letters were arranged in a long column. Patrick examined the first few rows.

```
AAAAA . . . A
AAAAB . . . B
AAABA . . . C
```

Emily had come up to stand beside him. "What's that?"

"I haven't a clue."

"Very well. I'm *leaving* now."

Outside, he heard more footsteps. Could Mr. Rockwell be finished already?

There was only one door. One way out. Emily was reaching out for the handle when she, too, heard the noise. She stared back at Patrick, her eyes filled with fear.

"Quick," he whispered, pointing to the wardrobe. "In here!"

Emily folded over her complicated hat and climbed into the nearly empty wardrobe. Patrick followed and they sat facing each other, their knees and the toes of their shoes touching, as he closed the door.

The lock clicked open. Someone entered. Breathing heavily, he shut the door behind him and exhaled with what sounded like relief.

Patrick heard him mutter the words "slovenly oaf" and then the sound of dishes and clothes being sorted. The voice didn't sound like Mr. Rockwell's. And why would a man call himself a slovenly oaf?

Emily's breathing was short. He felt her shaking and should have reached out to take her hand but he couldn't summon the courage. What seemed like twenty minutes passed before the cleaning and sorting stopped. Mr. Rockwell, or whoever it was, paused. A dish crashed and shattered. There was a click, reminiscent of a valise's lock snapping open, a few moments of shuffling, the rustling of clothes and then, finally, a low swoosh as the base of the cabin door brushed against the carpet.

Finally, the man was gone.

Emily climbed out first, her face colorless. She held her hat in shaking hands, counting her birds, smoothing the crease in the brim. Small beads of sweat had emerged on her colorless brow. "Please, let's get out of here."

"Agreed," Patrick answered, "but we should wait until he's down the hall."

His foot kicked against something beneath the bed. He hadn't seen it before: a heavily worn piece of luggage.

"I'm leaving," she urged.

"One more minute."

The valise held a neatly folded dinner jacket, shirt, and matching pants. Two pairs of carefully polished shoes. Another suit, slightly rumpled, a number of books. And, more important, a curly blond wig, a matching mustache, thin spectacles, and a long, sharp, double-sided blade with a silver medallion at the base in lieu of a handle.

He'd seen something like it before—his father had a small collection. These knives were used to cut open the bound pages of new books.

"Great, you found a book knife," Emily said. "Goodbye."

Normally these knives were dull, but when Patrick touched his finger to the blade, he started to bleed.

"I don't think this is meant for books."

Patrick pressed the small cut to the inside of his suit jacket and followed Emily out of the room. She was nearly sprinting. Patrick ran after her and, at the base of the stairs, glanced back as the strangely proportioned steward from the Reading and Writing Room emerged from a doorway.

TREASURE ISLAND'S HERO

"**D**o you understand what he means by that?" Harry asked. "I will say it again: 'Crafty men condemn studies, simple men admire them, and wise men use them.' Think, Patrick. What does he mean?"

The two sat across from one another in the Reading & Writing Room, and Harry had already drunk down three cups of coffee. He was serious about this tutoring arrangement. Patrick, on the other hand, was preoccupied. In the last hour alone, he had broken into Rockwell's room, discovered that the man, or some accomplice, was harboring a dangerous weapon, and nearly been caught—all in the company of a very perplexing girl. Think? How could he be expected to think?

What Patrick did know was that he wasn't ready to decide one way or the other. There was still time; Mr. Rockwell had requested that he bring him the book the following morning. Until then, he would not discuss a word of it with Harry.

"I repeat," Harry said, "wise men *use* them."

"Well," Patrick said at last, "I suppose he is saying that studies—"

"By which he means careful, courageous reading, not merely schoolroom concentration. Sorry, go on."

"He is saying that studies are not just for pleasure or leisure. They can be applied in the world."

"Precisely!"

"But . . ."

"What is it?"

"I suppose I'm wondering . . . wouldn't a man who studies a lot say that studying is useful?"

"No, but you see—" Harry stopped himself and stared into his gold-rimmed coffee cup. "Yes, yes, good point! We should not trust the lawyer to lecture us on the utility of the law. But I think you are wrong to consider Bacon a mere scholar. Don't forget, he was also a crafty man, if we consider his efforts to dismiss his own uncle to gain favor with the Queen."

Patrick didn't know enough about Bacon to argue the point, but he didn't agree with the notion that book knowledge was somehow powerful. James wouldn't agree either. Patrick wanted to prove that Harry was wrong, and the sight of *Treasure Island* prompted an idea.

"You said you love Stevenson, correct?"

"Completely."

"I don't think he would agree with Sir Francis or you," Patrick said, tapping the cover. "The hero of this story, the one who saves everyone and finds the treasure, is the resourceful man, the man of skills. The hero is Ben Gunn."

Harry raised his hands, palms out, as if he were deflecting the words. "No! No! No! The hero is Dr. Livesey. He is the one to whom young Jim appeals from the start, and he never disappoints!" Harry sipped his coffee, sat back, and crossed his arms on his chest. "You will recognize that one day when you're older."

Few replies could have been more insulting. "Of course. I am young, so I cannot possibly be right about anything," Patrick snapped.

Harry laid his hands flat, palms down, on the table and breathed in through his nose. With deep sincerity he replied, "I am sorry. That was wrong."

An apology? Patrick could hardly reply. He rarely met men who would admit when they were wrong. His father was one of the few.

"That said," Harry continued, "I do contend that you are wrong about *Treasure Island.*" Patrick started to speak, but Harry stopped him. "Back to our friend Bacon, if you will. In this same essay, Of Studies, he imparts another critical lesson: 'The general counsels, and the plots and marshaling of affairs, come best from those that are learned.' His point here is that the great leaders of men studied. You must study too, Patrick, if you hope to someday be a great man, a leader."

After years of his mother telling him he would amount to nothing at all, Patrick would have settled for growing up to be useful. But great? A leader? He had not even considered the notion.

"You do not need to be strong or fast. You do not need to be tall or handsome," Harry said, standing straight. He tucked in his chin, raised an eyebrow, then assumed a fighter's stance. "You need not possess a powerful right punch." Harry threw a mock right, pulled back his fist, and tapped Patrick's head with his finger. "To be great you need a sharp, trained mind! I can tell you that you have the capacity, Patrick. What you lack is the training."

A rattling noise diverted their attention. Cheverton, one of the younger stewards, was bearing a tray of rattling china and glaring his way. Only then did Patrick realize he was still seated. Harry had collected his books and was ready to go, yet Patrick remained in his chair as if he were the passenger. All this talk of being a great man had set his brain spinning. He jumped up, thankful that Mr. Webb had not seen him.

"I will leave you with the reprint. I would like you to study an essay of your choosing," he said, handing him the thin book. "Keep in mind another point of Bacon's while you do."

Staring down at the thin volume, Patrick asked, "What is that?"

"He said that some books are to be tasted, others to be swallowed, and some few to be chewed and digested."

A small bell rang. Cheverton had stepped out; the women were calling to Patrick. One of them was daintily jingling a small silver bell.

"Attend to the queens if you must," Harry said with a smile. "But remember that you are in my employ for the remainder of this voyage. I will be occupied for the rest of the afternoon and evening, but I expect you to spend your time reading."

At that point it was merely late afternoon. Probably not even three o'clock. "The whole night?"

Harry handed him another book. *Treasure Island.*

"But I told you," Patrick said, "I have already read this."

Tapping his finger on the green, hardened cloth cover, Harry said, "I have read this book thirty-one times and I still find new insights with each session. You do not have to read all night, of course. I would never deny a man his sleep. But I expect to have a rich conversation with you on the subject of these books tomorrow morning. I will call for you after church services." Harry started toward the door. "And Patrick?"

"Yes, Harry?"

"Chew carefully."

THE KNIFE WOULD NOT SUFFICE

The card had been sitting before him, propped against the stem of a wine goblet, for at least five minutes, but Mr. Rockwell failed to notice it until he'd picked away every sinew of meat from the roasted stuffed duckling before him. Berryman should have known to wait until Mr. Rockwell had finished his plate, or even his entire dinner, but he was desperate for direction.

At last, Mr. Rockwell picked up the card. Berryman expected a sign of frustration, even a brief flash of anger as Rockwell read the words—*The boy was in our cabin and the key to the cipher is gone*—but Rockwell displayed no evidence of distress. Instead he dabbed the corner of his mouth with his napkin. He placed his hands on the table, seemingly ready to push back. Perhaps he was merely concealing his anger. Perhaps he'd vent in the privacy of their cabin.

Before Rockwell could stand, however, a waiter appeared beside him with a silver-hooded plate. A stillness came over him. The hood was dramatically removed. He lifted knife and fork and began to eat.

Berryman brushed a fingertip against each end of his prominent mustache, checked to see that his stomach was centered. What was he supposed to do now? Rockwell had already insisted that he give up his plans to arrange for Harry's suicide, claiming that he did not want to make a scene. But he had been certain that Rockwell, upon reading the note, would demand action. In fact, he assumed that Rockwell would ask him to dispose of the young spittoon-carrying steward.

Berryman had even decided how he would carry out the regrettable but necessary task. His beautifully sharpened book knife would have been the preferred instrument, but the interior of *Titanic* was quite simply too white. The splatter of blood resulting from a fatal stab or slice would be terrible—it would torture him to see those clean halls stained. No, the knife would not suffice. He would question the boy, discover what plans had been set in motion without their knowledge, demand the key to the cipher, and then push the runt over the rail and into the dark cold water below. He wouldn't even have to bother with a suicide note. Nobody would miss the pest.

Now, however, his slovenly partner appeared to be in no hurry to recover the cipher or exterminate the boy. Could he not see that this was absolutely necessary? Berryman busily marched into the galley, passed the hot press, stepped into a small, dark, refrigerated room and closed the door behind him. He needed to think. But what was that smell? He was overwhelmed by brine, an odor reminiscent of low tide near a wide bay. He switched on the light and revealed that he'd taken refuge in a storage room for oysters. It smelled, but it would do.

Berryman reviewed the recent events. Rockwell had told the boy of his plans and proposed some incredibly generous terms. But Waters had no intention of accepting this contract. By chance Berryman had turned back after leaving their cabin earlier that afternoon, and he spied Waters and a young girl emerging from the room. He followed them, but they did not go straight to Widener. Berryman then intended to return to the cabin to check to see if anything was missing, but a pair of stewards demanded his help with an older man who had fallen ill. He had to oblige, not out of sympathy for the spoiled wretch, but because he had to maintain the illusion that he was a steward. Later, when he did return to the cabin, he discovered that the key to the cipher was gone.

He could only assume that Waters had stolen it. The boy had probably told Widener all he knew. Widener would scour the book and use the key to discover the formula himself. The wealthy young man would grow wealthier still, while he, John Francis Berryman, would remain unjustly mired in debt.

He breathed in through his nose, inhaling the brine. The great remaining question centered on Rockwell's indifference. How could his partner react so blithely? Stood up next to his order to let Harry live, this pointed to only one conclusion: Rockwell and Widener had formed an alliance. Berryman was the one to be tossed overboard, not Harry Widener.

Berryman did not want to believe it. True, Rockwell had not been an ideal partner; he was too stingy with his money, reluctant to advance Berryman more than a few pounds at a time despite all the work he had done. But until that moment he had not considered the possibility that the oaf might deceive him.

From that point forward, Berryman decided, he would have to act alone, with only his interests in mind. There was no use confronting Rockwell directly. He'd be better off maintaining the ruse, pretending all was well with their partnership, and that he had not a clue that Rockwell had turned against him.

But he did need more information to formulate a proper plan. He had to act. Berryman had to question the boy, find out what he knew. Then, once he had extracted this information, he would dispose of him.

With conviction he emerged from the oyster room and nearly collided with the head steward, Mr. Webb. He mumbled an apology and pushed on, but Webb stopped him.

"Who are you?"

Berryman invented a name. "Bowden, sir. Theodore Bowden."

"You're not one of my staff."

"No, sir, second-class steward, here to help—"

"Back where you belong, Mr. Bowden. If I need help I will ask for it."

"Of course, sir," he replied, "I'll return straightaway."

Supremely bothered, he hurried to Rockwell's cabin, slipped the book knife inside his coat, checked his paunch and mustache in the mirror, and proceeded to search the boat for Waters. Webb seemed like the sort who would try to verify the name he'd offered, so, to be safe, this would be the last time Berryman made use of the disguise. Once he found the boy and completed his task he'd hurl the lot into the sea.

Unfortunately, finding Waters proved far more difficult than he expected. After searching for an hour or more, he concluded that the boy had gone to sleep. The stewards' bunk rooms were amidships, on the port side. Senior stewards such as Mr. Webb enjoyed cabins, but the lesser workers crammed together. Thankfully, Berryman took his rest in Rockwell's cabin; a sofa in a first-class cabin was easily preferable to such plebian quarters. Inside, the bright, low moon illuminated the bunks, casting bluish light on the faces of the soundly sleeping men. Not one of them stirred.

Berryman reached inside his jacket to finger the long,

gleaming blade and found that his right hand was shaking. He clenched the cloth in his pocket to quiet his quivering hand. He'd use the knife to draw the boy out of the bunks, question him, then employ the cloth to stifle his inevitable scream.

The act itself would be fleeting. He would strike and run. Even if someone were to spot him, he would be safe, as he would quickly discard the disguise. Perhaps he would then join the others in their search for the murderer.

First, though, he did have to find the boy. But where was he? Berryman must have searched every bunk twice.

A gruff Scotsman angrily awoke. "What's your business?" he growled. "Can't we be allowed some peace?"

Berryman bowed and left without a word. This Waters boy was truly beginning to bother him.

21

AN INFERIOR CREATURE

While Berryman was hunting, Patrick was sitting upright on a mattress in the trimmers' bunks, propped against the wall and chewing as instructed. That afternoon he had spent an hour searching for a good place to chew. He tried several mess halls, a section of the Boat Deck where crew members were allowed to take the air, an infrequently used stairwell, and even the wireless room. The operators, Harold Bride and Jack Philips, kindly invited him to sit and read.

Yet none of these spots were right. Another member of the crew would inevitably pass by and scold him. Some would even yell or curse: "Put down your fairy tale and get back to work!"

Explaining that in fact he was working, that he had actually been assigned the task of spending that evening slowly chewing and digesting those two books, was far too much trouble, so each time he was questioned or yelled at he would simply close his books and move on. Eventually he thought of the trimmers' bunks, and it proved ideal. The men were so exhausted when they slumped in that they didn't even ask him to switch off the light above his bunk.

This lack of distraction was welcome because Bacon's book was incredibly difficult. Patrick wasn't even chewing the essays, really. He was nibbling off the bottom right corner of an *a*, the dot of an *i*, but little more. There was wisdom in the man's words, no doubt, but Patrick had to read and think slowly to understand any of it. Nothing was spelled normally—*s* was written as *f*, but so was the actual *f*—so each word was like a puzzle in and of itself.

Treasure Island, on the other hand, was a joy, a delightful relief from the debate he'd been conducting in his head about whether to help Mr. Rockwell. Patrick nearly read the whole book through. In the years since his father died and his mother effectively had banned his books, Patrick had forgotten how much he loved those characters. Young Jim Hawkins in particular was a marvel. At the start he saves his mother. Then he's the first to learn of Long John Silver's plot. Later he fends off the duplicitous sea cook, cuts the ship free to prevent the pirates' escape, and sails himself away from certain death.

Jim is also the one who discovers Ben Gunn, the sailor who had been abandoned on the island years before. And Gunn clearly becomes the key figure in the story, not Dr. Livesey, as Harry insisted. Patrick's reading only confirmed what he'd said before. Granted, Dr. Livesey does organize the quest and lead the resistance to the mutiny. But without Ben Gunn, Dr. Livesey and the rest would have been left with nothing. Their grand quest would have been a failure!

"At our leisure, are we?"

Patrick snapped the book shut. "Martin?" His brother's friend was already lying on his back. "How is James?"

Blaney coughed, wheezed, wiped coal-dust-streaked sweat from his brow. "While you are up here reading your little novels—"

"No, no, I have to read them," Patrick started, but there was no use continuing. Blaney wouldn't accept that this was work. Nor would James.

"All I see is a boy who came here to work but behaves like he's first-class himself," Blaney wheezed. "Your brother would be disgusted."

"Where is he?" Patrick asked. He had to see James immediately, to explain himself before he heard it from someone else. He would die if James thought he was lazy. "Where's my brother?" he asked again.

"You didn't hear?"

"Hear what?"

"Your brother has been working three days straight on nearly no rest. The coal finally got the better of him."

"What? What do you mean?"

"James is in hospital. He is not well."

Patrick grabbed his books and raced up two different sets of stairs to C Deck, through a hall beside the crew galley, and then down the double-wide steps leading to the third-class common room. The space was vast and open, but sparsely furnished. He cut between men smoking in small groups, children playing on the floor, and quickened his pace when he reached the long passageway the crew referred to as Scotland Road. Someone called to him but he did not stop. He had to see his brother.

Thankfully, as Mr. Webb had told him, *Titanic* had only the best medical facilities and surgeons. Advanced machines stood tall in the corners and numerous glass-door cabinets were packed with bottles of medicine.

An attendant heard him rumble down the steps. "Can I help you?" she asked.

"I'm looking for my brother, James Waters."

A doctor leaned out of an office, then stepped forward and extended his hand. "Is that a Belfast accent? James Simpson, assistant surgeon, born in Belfast. Yourself too I presume?"

"Yes, Cargill Street. But listen, I'm looking—"

"Cargill! I know it well. Now how can we help you?"

"My brother . . . James Waters . . . he has been working on putting out the fire—"

"Shhhh! We are not to be talking about that fire, my friend. Captain's orders and such. Is your brother a thick man, strong?"

"Yes, that's him."

"He's not here. I looked after him myself, administered a measure of paregoric to ease the cough and help him rest. He'll be in the crew hospital."

"But . . . I was told these are the best facilities on board."

"They are, of course, but they are only for passengers. Don't fear, though. The head surgeon and I give every man and woman, passenger or crew, equal attention. I assure you."

The crew hospital, he soon found out, was just above the trimmers' bunks. Patrick had run right past it on his way, and when he arrived there a few minutes later, James was lying on his back, hands folded on his chest, like a dead man in a casket.

"James? James, it's me, Patrick."

His brother said nothing. A nurse suggested that it would be best not to disturb him, so Patrick sat on the edge of the thin mattress and watched him sleep. His face, wiped free of coal and sweat, looked pale and thin, almost blue in places, and his breathing was steady but difficult. The deep wheeze with each breath sounded like a distant, low accordion.

The mattress was wafer-like, the sheets as coarse as burlap. This was his brother! This was James Waters! He did not deserve to be in a second-class hospital. Especially not after working himself nearly to death down in that boiler room. He should have been cared for like a king.

Patrick was still clutching Harry's books. He placed them on a small side table and regarded them bitterly. If Harry Widener or one of his class had so much as a sniffle, the ship's medical staff would probably assign him his very own doctor. Yet a member of the crew was treated like an inferior creature.

The reason was money. The ship, his life, the entire world —at the heart of it all was money. If you had it, you could flourish. If you did not, they would treat you like a horse and work you until you could work no more. Patrick could not change the world, but he could start trying to change his place in it. And his brother's, too. Fifty pounds would not make them Wideners, but it would be a start.

He was going to steal Harry's book.

STEALING FROM THE STEAM ROOM

Sunday morning on *Titanic* was no time for rest and quiet, as it was back in Belfast. The ship was busy as ever. Patrick spent his morning polishing the Smoking Room's silver, then headed for the Turkish baths. Harry, he learned, would be enjoying the baths following church services, and he hoped to arrive shortly after his tutor.

He waited, hiding around the corner from the entrance, until he saw Harry approach, ticket in hand, and enter the baths. The leather case containing the Bacon was at his side. Once the door closed, Patrick pressed his ear to the tempered glass. He heard the attendant, in a London accent, tell Harry to leave his belongings and follow him.

A few minutes later, Patrick crept inside. The floors and walls were inlaid with radiant blue and green tiles, the mosaics were splendid, the light fixtures exotic. He heard there were hot rooms, steam rooms, cooling rooms, even rooms dedicated solely to shampooing. There were lounges everywhere, but luckily the room was empty save for a man in a blue robe. He was lying on his back with a white towel covering his face.

Across the way Patrick spotted the dressing rooms. His breathing was short; he could feel the blood pulsing faster through his neck. The argument he'd made to Emily, the idea that it wasn't theft if he returned the book, now struck him as weak.

But it was the only way. With the money from Rockwell he could ensure that his brother received the best medical treatment possible. James could then find a less demanding job. He would never have to feel the burn of the boilers on his face again.

Harry's clothes hung neatly in the first booth. A wave of doubt rolled through Patrick: Would his tutor really leave the book here? He didn't see it at first and experienced a kind of relief. But then, beneath the short wooden bench, he saw the familiar case propped up against the far wall, covered in shadow.

Without another thought Patrick removed the rare edition and replaced it with the reprint. They were the same shape and weight; the case truly felt no different. If Harry took it out he would know immediately, but Patrick hoped he could prevent him from doing so, for a while at least. He would interrupt Harry on his way out of the baths and assault him with questions about

Treasure Island. He could keep Harry talking for an hour or more, after which Mr. Rockwell would return the book. As for switching them back . . . he could devise a way to do that later.

Patrick held the second edition face up in his widespread palm. He had to go. He had to rush the book to Mr. Rockwell.

But he couldn't move. The very sight of the *Essaies* was paralyzing. The brittle edges, the centuries-old creases and wrinkles in the paper—one wrong move would inflict permanent damage. His heart pounded harder. What if he tripped? What if he accidentally ripped or stained the book? Even if he did manage to deliver it undamaged, Mr. Rockwell didn't strike him as the sort who would treat a rare book with the proper care. A teardrop of gravy might fall from his chin. Even the slightest stain would horrify Harry.

And a betrayal, Patrick guessed, would devastate him. He'd placed his trust in Patrick. This was no way to repay him. Patrick reached down to return the Bacon to its case, but he had delayed too long.

"Patrick?"

He turned. Red-faced and wrapped in a robe, Harry stood before him. He looked from the leather case to Patrick and back.

"I was just—"

"Patrick? What in God's name are you doing with the Bacon?"

A SMOLDERING BOOK

Harry led the way up to the Boat Deck with Patrick following glumly a step behind. Although his tutor had cooled and dressed, his face was still red from the steam. Patrick's was red from shame as he told Harry about James, Mr. Rockwell, the strange disguises, and the promise of fifty pounds.

Harry's first words were stern and simple. "Injustice is no cause for theft," he said. "And I am inclined to believe you, but I'm not certain another man in my position would do the same."

"I swear," Patrick pleaded. "I was returning it. I realized it was wrong."

Harry stopped at the rail. He leaned pensively on his forearms, then turned and straightened. "You are not a thief, Patrick. I know you are good; easily misguided, apparently, but essentially good. Still, I am disappointed," he said. "Supremely disappointed."

Harry turned again and stared out at the gray ocean. There was nothing Patrick could say. He joined his tutor at the rail.

"As for your brother," Harry continued, "I will see to it myself that he receives the best care possible, both during this voyage and after."

Patrick stared down at the water. "Am I to lose my job?"

"Hardly, Patrick. We have more work to finish now than ever before."

"I don't deserve your help."

"No, Patrick, you misunderstand. This time you are going to help me. I suspect Mr. Rockwell is no Robin Hood, despite what he says; but I would like to find out if he's right about my book. To do so, we'll have to study the *Essaies* in an entirely new way." Harry paused, then added, "You say he has an accomplice?"

"I think so, yes."

"Then we will require a safe place to work as well. My stateroom would be too obvious a choice. You know this ship. Could you suggest someplace they won't think to look?"

"I have the perfect spot," Patrick answered, and walked toward the bow.

Inside the wireless room, the operators were frantically tapping away messages and in no mood to entertain. Once Harry produced a pair of fine cigars, however, Bride happily cleared them a desk.

Harry removed a few pieces of stationery from his leather case, laid them on the table, and handed Patrick a pencil. "To make notes as you read," he explained.

The paper was large, thick, and white, with "HEW" stamped into the top. Patrick held it up admiringly.

"Almost too nice to sully with a pencil stroke, isn't it? It's Whatman's handmade, the finest paper there is, in my opinion. But please, it is made for writing, so do not hesitate."

"What am I supposed to write? What are we looking for?"

"To be honest, I do not know, Patrick. It would be reasonable to presume, based on Mr. Rockwell's talk of hidden information, that the text harbors a secret message of some sort. Bacon was fond of such tricks. To find it, we must examine the words, the type, every graphic element of every page," Harry explained. "A misspelled word or an extra curl or two in a cursive letter could harbor a critical clue."

"But Bacon spells everything strangely," Patrick noted, Even the title of the book—*Essaies.*

"Yes, yes, I know, but I'm very familiar with the grammatical and stylistic conventions of this time period, so I should be able to spot any intentional deviations from the norm. Why don't you focus on the illustrated elements, and I'll concentrate on the text?"

Patrick studied the volume until his eyes burned and teared. They spent at least a few minutes on every page. Four hours passed before they reached the end. Harry sat back, exhaled with a smile and pulled a gold watch from his pocket.

Mistaking the smile for success, Patrick asked, "You see something?"

"No!" Harry said excitedly. "But we are not up against some petty puzzler here, Patrick. This is the great Sir Francis Bacon! We will need more than a few hours to discover his secret." He collected the book and his stationery and stood. "Have some food and meet me back here after dinner. You won't mind, will you, gents?" Harry asked, raising his voice.

"Another cigar and that desk is yours for the duration," Bride answered.

"You will have a box," Harry declared. "If you happen to see Mr. Rockwell," he added to Patrick, "affirm your commitment. Tell him I'd locked the Bacon away or some such excuse and that you plan to secure it in the morning. And eat well, Patrick. Our work has merely begun."

In a fog Patrick descended several decks to Scotland Road, heading for the stewards' mess hall. He tucked the replica of the *Essaies* into his waistband, under his suit jacket, and it felt right to have a book with him. A few days earlier he would not have admitted it, but he missed books and stories. He wanted to follow his brother, but Patrick was a reader, not a trimmer. He wasn't a tough, stone-cut Kelly. He was a tall, swaying, thoughtful descendant of the Waters line who preferred puzzling over a strange book to laboring with his hands. He knew that now, and he had Harry to thank.

Suddenly someone palmed Patrick's head and bounced it off a steel doorframe. The scene swayed; his eyes blacked out.

"The book!" his attacker hissed. "Give it to me."

Patrick's vision cleared enough to make out a blade in the yellow white light. He was standing, but barely. He threw his hand against the wall to steady himself.

His attacker was dressed like a passenger.

"I don't have it," Patrick pleaded.

"Liar! I saw you looking at it only a moment ago. I'd like the book, the key, and an explanation, and I'd like them now."

Two second-class stewards stepped out of the lavatory and into the hall. The man backed off, hiding the knife, and without a moment's hesitation Patrick sprinted away. If he didn't lose his attacker in the maze, he'd exhaust him on the succession of stairs.

But his attacker proved resilient. He was a mere ten yards away at the first set of steps, and by the time Patrick had reached C Deck, the man was gaining. Patrick had barely swung closed the door and crossed the hall to descend again when his attacker arrived at the top. Patrick took the steps three and four at a time, then cut across to the winding stairs down to the firemen's passage. There was no need to look up: He could hear the man's boots clanging louder and louder on the metal steps above.

His head cleared but still rang with pain. Down in the belly of *Titanic* the noise and heat intensified, the thumping turbines shaking his very core. At the end of the firemen's passage, he dodged a few trimmers slinging coal and made it to the bunker in boiler room number five.

Blaney was working alongside Dickson, a strong-armed Southampton trimmer. Patrick waited within arms' reach of the boiler, holding out the book. Now that he'd stopped, he could feel the painful pounding in his head. He gently dabbed the spot with his fingers; it was extremely sore, but not bleeding.

His attacker finally caught up and stopped a few steps away, breathing hard. The stowaway! His clothes were different, but Patrick was sure it was the same man. Now he was buttoned up in a dinner jacket, with his brown hair flattened forward and wire-rimmed glasses that suggested intelligence.

"Thief!" the stowaway called out.

The trimmers and stokers ignored him and continued shoveling coal.

"I have stolen nothing," Patrick replied.

"Do they have a deal, the two of them? What have they promised you?" he asked, moving closer.

Patrick removed the book and held it close to the fiery maw of the boiler. "You're the one who is working with Mr. Rockwell, aren't you?"

The stowaway's demeanor changed completely. "Please," he begged, "don't do that!"

"You were disguised when you stole the book that night in the Smoking Room."

The man continued pleading, "You can't destroy it . . . that book . . ."

"What about it? What are you looking for?"

Without answering the stowaway lunged forward to grab it, but Patrick quickly flicked it atop the glowing coals.

The intense heat set it ablaze immediately.

"NO!"

The stowaway ripped Dickson's shovel out of his hands and dug out the burning book. Stunned, the strong-armed trimmer threw him to the floor.

Blaney picked up his own iron rod and the two men stood over the fallen stowaway.

The book lay on the floor, cover down, smoldering.

"Please!" the stowaway shouted. "Extinguish that fire, please! I'll pay you in gold!"

As Blaney glanced down at the burning book, the man kicked his legs out from beneath him. Then he jumped to his feet and stomped repeatedly on the *Essaies* before Blaney swung his rod into the man's shoulder, knocking him aside.

The stowaway wailed, and nearly fell. Patrick backed away, watching as the man reached into his jacket and removed a long, gleaming knife—the same one Patrick had inspected in Mr. Rockwell's cabin. The man's arm was undoubtedly bruised, if not broken, but he swung his good one, slashing out at the trimmers with the blade.

Blaney and Dickson, wielding their iron shovels like maces, smirked, as though they were being threatened with a teaspoon. Yet they moved no closer.

The stowaway stared down at the charred book, then at Patrick. A change came over him. He was angry now, not desperate. "They have it already, don't they? Harry and that duplicitous oaf—they'll share the spoils of the formula?"

"What do you mean?" Patrick asked. "What formula?"

"You care to tell us what is happening here, Waters?" Blaney pressed.

"They'll cheat you, too, boy!" the stowaway yelled. Then he glanced behind him, saw that the path was clear, and ran.

THE KEY TO THE CIPHER

Patrick spent the evening in the crew hospital, sitting by his brother's bed. James stirred occasionally, coughed and turned, but never fully awoke. After the confrontation in the boiler room, Blaney and Dickson had enlisted Chief Engineer Bell and assured Patrick that the stowaway would be found. But he was not terribly confident. The man had avoided capture at least once already. Yet Patrick did feel safe there in the crew hospital, beside his brother.

Now that he'd burned the replica of the *Essaies*, though, he could not finish his assignment. He had no choice but to continue poring through *Treasure Island*. This second reading session was very different from the first. Slowly, begrudgingly, he had begun to change his opinion on the matter of the novel's true hero.

The book practically demanded that he agree with Harry. He chose chapters and sections at random, but nearly every one, whether the man was present in the scene or not, suggested that Harry was right about Dr. Livesey. When Jim and his mother flee the Admiral Benbow Inn, they go straight to Livesey. The doctor then organizes the quest. When Long John Silver, the sea cook, turns out to be a mutinous rogue, it is Livesey who stands up to the one-legged fiend. If not the captain of the ship, he is undoubtedly the leader of the expedition.

There was no use contesting the fact that Harry was right: Dr. Livesey, the man of knowledge, was the crucial figure in the story. Ben Gunn might be the one who uncovers the treasure, but without Livesey, he never would've known how to find it.

At nine o'clock Patrick closed the book, left a note beside his brother's bed, and met Harry in the wireless office. He traveled only through passenger halls and stairways to avoid meeting Rockwell's agent.

The promised box of cigars sat on one counter and Harry was watching Bride when Patrick arrived. "Fascinating, Patrick! Imagine how well this wireless system works: Officer Bride here is actually receiving warnings from nearby ships about fields of ice in the area. And I've just sent a missive to one of my book agents in New York!"

Bride acknowledged Patrick with a quick wave and got back to his work. Beside him, Phillips was busy with a tangle of wires.

Patrick set *Treasure Island* on the table.

"And the Bacon?"

"I'm sorry," Patrick answered, and told Harry the story of Rockwell's accomplice.

After a moment Harry asked, "You are certain he said formula?"

"Completely certain."

"What sort of formula, I wonder?"

Recalling his first meeting with Mr. Rockwell, out on the deck, Patrick reminded Harry of the nail and the shilling.

Harry lifted a fist to his chin and smiled. "It couldn't be alchemy."

"I don't remember Rockwell using that word, but the man in the boiler rooms definitely said something about a formula."

"Ha! Delightful. I confess, I'm hardly a believer, but through the years many have sought the power of alchemy, the ability to transform any metal into gold. I doubt Bacon would have discovered it, given that history suggests he died in debt, but it would be fascinating, wouldn't it? Imagine—the power to simply *make* gold. You would need a formula to do so, I imagine."

The notion was impossible to fathom. To Patrick, fifty pounds was an outlandish sum. But *making* gold? That could lead to a thousand pounds. A million!

Harry shook his head, stifling his smile. "We should be safe enough to work here for now, though I'll see to some extra precautions for ourselves and the book. You're more familiar with the ship; can you think of a good, safe place to hide my little Bacon?"

There were a thousand spots, maybe more. But if he were to stash the book somewhere, he wouldn't tuck it into a corner or place it high on a shelf. He'd give it to the one person he trusted above all else on that boat, even if he was stuck in bed. "Yes," Patrick said at last, "I do."

"Good, then let's turn to the task before us."

"Wait," Patrick said. "I wanted to talk about *Treasure Island* first. You were right about Dr. Livesey, and I would like to explain why I have changed my mind."

Harry laughed. "Interesting, interesting, but let's not dwell on *Treasure Island* now. We must focus on the Bacon."

The book was resting on a cloth, the bottom of the page aligned with the edge of the table. Harry had a cup of coffee with him, but he held it on his lap and leaned away when he sipped, careful not to spill a drop near the book.

Bride peered over them, drinking from a cup of his own.

"Careful!" Harry declared.

"The book is very rare," Patrick explained. "He's worried that you'll spill."

"Oh, no bother!" Bride said, and set the cup down on a different counter. "Now, what's the mystery here?"

"Patrick," Harry said, "why don't you explain our little story? Leave out the villains, of course."

"You can't leave out the villains!" Bride said. "They're the best part of any story."

"But they won't help us here. Patrick?"

"We are looking for a formula, hidden in code. These villains—"

"Aha!" Bride said. "You can't leave out the villains!"

"Right," Patrick said. "These villains are also eager to acquire this particular copy."

"But it is mine," Harry noted.

"Bride!" Philips shouted. "We're getting more ice warnings."

"Yes, one moment!" The operator stared down at the now open book. "What about the inscription?" he asked, pointing at the handwritten note on the first page. "Surely that's unique to this copy."

Patrick examined the handwritten note closely:

Loving and beloved brother,
Riches are for spending, and ſpending
for honour & good actions.
                    F Bacon

He studied Harry's face as Bride moved back to his desk. Was it that simple? "Harry?" Patrick asked, "Do you think he's right?"

His tutor's face was pale, his jaw slack. Then the color rose in his cheeks and he clapped his hands. "Yes! I've been wondering why Bacon chose to quote that particular line in his note to his brother, but it's perfectly sensible now. Even obvious! He's telling Anthony to go ahead and spend the money wisely! How could we not have seen this? You are a genius, Mr. Bride!"

The wireless operator was already too busy to respond.

"We'll send that gentleman a room full of fine cigars. Now, look closely, Patrick, and tell me what you see."

A few words were spelled strangely, but Harry had already explained that this was the style of the day; the entire book was written this way. The letter *f* was often really an *s*. The *u* in *louing* was actually a *v*.

The words also ran at an angle, not straight in line with the page. But that wouldn't mean anything. The only other oddity —and he couldn't be sure, exactly—was that in a few cases it almost looked like Bacon's handwriting changed from one letter to the next. He pointed this out to Harry.

"Brilliant, Patrick!" he said. Harry reached over and tapped him on the head. "I told you there's a fine mind in there! The words here are a distraction. They encode the real message via the Baconian cipher, a method the great man developed himself."

"How does it work? Can you read what it really says?"

"Yes, well, it's not that easy. I use codes myself, in my ledger of book purchases, so I do have some experience in the field. As I recall, depending on which one of two typefaces he used for each letter or, in this case, which style of handwriting, we assign either an A or a B."

"The cursive gets the A or the plain print?"

"The plainly written letter, I believe."

Patrick took a piece of Harry's stationery and began working it out. The first word – Louing—became ABAABA because the first letter was straight, standard print, the second written in flowing cursive, the third and forth back to the standard form, and so forth.

"What now?" he asked. "What do the letters mean?"

Harry's thin eyebrows arched. "I wish I could say, but I don't know."

Patrick should have guessed it wouldn't be that simple.

Harry pointed to the original inscription. "If this message is the vault, and our sequence of As and Bs the lock, we're still lacking something."

"The key."

"Precisely. We need the key to translate these sequences and reveal the secret. The Baconian cipher, as I recall, has a fairly simple key, but I confess, I don't remember quite how it goes."

"I thought you remember everything you read."

"Normally I do!"

Patrick stared at the sequence of As and Bs. He'd seen something like that before. But where?

"What is it, Patrick?" Harry asked.

The wireless apparatus popped, accompanied by a curse from Bride. Patrick's mind cleared: Mr. Rockwell's desk. That column of paper.

"Why are you smiling?" Harry asked.

"I think I know where to find the key."

THE INCAPABLE ACADEMIC

The cold night air pressed against his flushed face, but the chill failed to penetrate through to Mr. Rockwell's core. Searing hot coffee swished in his stomach, warming his insides. He hardly needed his coat.

His Sunday evening dinner had been delightful. Indeed, Mr. Rockwell should have been a happy man. But he was not.

First, the boy had disappointed him. The elephant-eared idiot remained loyal to his book-collecting friend and failed to deliver the *Essaies* at the appointed time. Then, when Mr. Rockwell sent Berryman in search of him, the incapable academic, who had begun acting even more oddly than usual, disappeared. At least five hours had passed, yet he still had not yet returned. Mr. Rockwell would have to develop a new strategy.

He had to set his nimble mind to this task immediately, as

only a few days remained before they'd arrive in New York. After that, Widener would bring the book back to his servant-stocked mansion. Procuring it at that point would be impossible.

Someone tapped him twice on the left shoulder; probably a steward, rudely interrupting his pleasant thoughts. "Thank you, but I require nothing," he said without looking.

"You've struck a deal with him, haven't you? You've already found the formula?"

Berryman, dressed as a passenger and insecure as always, glared at him defiantly.

"Where have you been?" Rockwell whispered. "A deal? With Widener? Certainly not." In the dim light Mr. Rockwell saw that Berryman's face was twisted with pain, but he felt no sympathy; they had a task to accomplish. "What happened to you now?" he demanded.

"Don't play the fool," Berryman hissed. "I know you're in league with Widener. I saw the book burn. Did you plan to have those beasts in the boiler room kill me? Did you pay them to toss—"

"Burn? Which book burned?"

"The *Essaies*, you oaf! I imagine you've worked it all out already. But I'm here to tell you that you will not cut me out of our arrangement, Archibald."

Berryman turned and a deck lamp illuminated his face. Rockwell could see that his eyes were wide and red. He was crazed, spouting conspiratorial nonsense. The very idea . . . Harry Widener would never allow one of his precious books to burn. He had to soothe the man. "John, my friend, please," Mr. Rockwell said, "I ordered no one to kill you!" This was a fact, but the idea was appealing, given Berryman's behavior. He would only be a liability from this point forward. "What you need is rest," he continued, wondering if he could find someone to apprehend the scholar in his sleep. "Go back to our cabin. Take my bed."

Berryman stared past him and hunched forward, hiding behind Mr. Rockwell's impressive frame. If Rockwell could simply convince Berryman to return to the room, he could then alert an officer to the fact that there was an intruder in his cabin. Berryman would be locked away and he could continue with the project unencumbered.

"I'm not that gullible, Archibald," Berryman answered, glancing again over his shoulder. "I'll be watching you." He pulled open his coat to reveal the knife. "You will not cheat me."

"Oh, put that away, you melodramatic fool! I've told you, there is no deal! And I'm certain the book is in fine condition. Harry Widener would never let it burn. Trust me, Berryman, we will soon be reclining upon thrones of gold."

Rage swept across Berryman's dark face. Mr. Rockwell turned to discover its source: The Waters boy stood an arm's length away.

Mr. Rockwell cast him a disarming smile. "Patrick! Good of you to join us. Do you have our book?"

"Mr. Widener requests a meeting with you in the Smoking Room."

Now Berryman grabbed Rockwell's sleeve threateningly.

"No deal, Archibald? You thieving—"

"THERE IS NO DEAL!" He pulled his arm free. "What does he want, Patrick?"

"He wants to meet with the both of you."

26

SUDDENLY, ODDLY SILENT

At a table in a quiet corner of the Smoking Room, Harry sat with his legs stretched out before him, reading. He closed the book as Rockwell, his accomplice, and Patrick approached and pointed to two empty chairs across from him. Patrick was happy to stand. The man with Rockwell, the stowaway, made him want to run.

Yet Harry wasn't frightened by him at all. In fact he smiled upon seeing him up close, his eyes wide with surprise. "John Berryman? Is that you?"

"You know him?" Patrick asked. "This is the man who has been trying to steal the book."

Harry ignored him. "I'd heard you were an academic, Berryman . . . is that right?"

Wiping his sweating brow with a clean white dinner napkin, Berryman stammered, "Yes . . . I . . ."

The ship became suddenly, oddly silent. Patrick's whole body felt the change.

Across the room one of the men said, "They've shut down the engines." The steady, deep hum that had formed a kind of background music to every moment aboard had ceased.

Berryman's brows arched and he centered himself. "Listen to me, Harry, I'm not the weak boy you once knew."

Harry shrugged, then replied, "Weak? I thought you were quite impressive. Remember our Shakespeare seminar?" Harry addressed Patrick. "The man's knowledge of the bard was astounding!"

"You . . . you remember that?"

"Your performance in the Lotos Eaters was remarkable, too. Oh, your costume!"

Now Berryman smiled. "Thank you, I—"

"Are you still wearing costumes now, Berryman? Dressing up as stewards and waiters?"

Harry pulled a canvas sack up from the floor and shook its contents out onto the table. A pair of wigs, eyeglasses, mustaches, and more. "Some associates of mine found these in your cabin, Rockwell—" he eyed the man's girth "—but I doubt you are capable of disguising your immensity, so I assume these must be yours, Berryman."

Berryman opened his mouth to reply, but produced no words. His face was blank, slack, his mind obviously steaming behind it. His eyes shot from Rockwell to Harry and back as he jabbed a finger at one and then the other. "I *know* what you two are trying to do," he said, "and I will not allow it."

Unintimidated, Harry shook his head at someone on the other side of the room.

A powerful but subtle shift in the floor caused Patrick to tilt to his left, as if he were poised to faint. But no . . . he was fine. The others seemed to have experienced the sway as well. There was a room-wide pause in conversation.

"Berryman, please," Mr. Rockwell cut in, "allow Mr. Widener and I to converse like gentlemen."

"No, Archibald, I deserve—"

"You are to call me, Mr. Rockwell—"

"NO! I'll call you what I like, you . . . you overstuffed omnivorous penguin. I should be handling these negotiations, *Archibald*. I'm the one who has done the work."

"My sincere congratulations for your hard work, Berryman, but this world of ours is not a meritocracy."

"Go order yourself a second dinner!" Berryman shouted back.

Patrick had enough. In a loud, firm voice he said, "Should we talk about Bacon's code?"

"Yes, we should," Harry said, clapping once, and forcefully. "Regardless of which one of you is the leader of your little outfit, you both should know that I have no intentions of surrendering my book, and that I have taken precautions to prevent you from acquiring it forcibly."

At this he nodded across the room, where two stewards stood watching. Patrick recognized them but couldn't recall their names. They were both large and strong, younger versions of Mr. Webb.

"What about the book?" Berryman pressed. "I watched it burn."

"A reprint," Patrick answered.

"I wouldn't be a very good teacher if my sole student showed so little respect for rare books, would I? Patrick set a 1904 edition ablaze. As I see it, gentlemen, you have two choices. We can all anxiously endure the rest of the voyage and I can look up the key to the cipher myself when I return home . . ."

Mr. Rockwell eagerly asked, "Or?"

"Or we act like civilized men. We cease the chasing and the threats—" he eyed Berryman "—and we reveal the secret together, like gentlemen."

Mr. Rockwell countered by laying a long strip of heavy paper face down on the table. "I am intrigued."

Patrick recognized it immediately from the cabin.

"The key to the cipher," Berryman said. "You had it all along."

"I have been carrying it with me since yesterday, as a precaution."

"But after all we've worked for, you cannot simply hand it over!"

"Please, gentlemen, calm yourselves," Harry interrupted. "Need I remind you that this key is no great secret? It is the only one on *Titanic*, but I could easily visit a library and look up the details myself when we reach New York."

Patrick had not considered this, but he saw that it was no surprise to Rockwell and Berryman.

"That said," Harry continued, "I would like to enjoy the remainder of our voyage, so I would prefer that we resolve this now." He looked at Berryman as if he were a misbehaving child. "Like Harvard gentlemen."

"What is your number, Widener?" Mr. Rockwell asked.

"Money? No, not for me, though I'm tempted to request enough for a Mazarin Bible," Harry said. "Patrick here will require one hundred pounds, which I believe is twice the amount you offered, Archibald."

"And for you?" Berryman asked.

"My interest is intellectual in nature. I'd like the opportunity to witness the attempt at alchemical transformation, the chance to see iron turn to gold. Above all else I'd like an assurance that you will leave my Bacon alone. If you agree not to touch it, I will gladly authorize a supervised reading."

Patrick studied his tutor's face. One hundred pounds would

be wonderful, but was Harry really not going to take any money at all?

Mr. Rockwell brought a fist down upon the table and shouted, "Deal!"

Berryman glared angrily at his partner, but Mr. Rockwell did not notice. He was thoroughly pleased and slipped the key to the cipher back inside his coat.

"Wonderful," Harry said. "Patrick, why don't you go get the *Essaies*? When you return, you will find us here or outside on the deck. I would like to know why they stopped the engines. Oh, and Patrick?"

"Yes Harry?"

"Do let him know that he will receive proper care."

Berryman glanced at Patrick, confused, as an excited passenger rushed into the Smoking Room. He was breathless and red in the face, his tie off-center. "Come see this!" he announced. "We've hit an iceberg!"

SWALLOWING WATER THROUGH THE BOW

Outside, several passengers were pointing astern, at the horizon. Patrick heard someone say the iceberg was visible, a dark mass back behind them, but he saw nothing. Harry went off to inquire about what had happened. Only an hour earlier he'd been dining with Captain Smith and the captain had boasted that the journey was going beautifully.

Mr. Rockwell, clearly feeling triumphant, dismissed the events and declared his intention to wait inside the Smoking Room with a strong cognac. The restless Berryman wandered off mumbling that he had something to see to, and that he would return in a few minutes.

As Patrick marched off to retrieve the book, he couldn't help looking behind him, slowing at every doorway or corner, fearing that Berryman would charge. Yes, they had a deal, but he did not trust that man.

"Patrick!" Emily said. "Have you heard?"

He had nearly walked into her. Too surprised to think clearly, struck by her unusually casual clothes, he said nothing. She wore a thick wool coat over a nightdress. Her hair wasn't bundled up at the back; it fell, long and thick and tangled, down over her shoulders. He stammered. "I . . . I was on my way . . ."

She pulled her coat tightly around her shoulders. "They said we've hit an iceberg. Isn't that exciting? Mother told me to remain in the room but of course I had to come see for myself."

He turned his head left and right. No sign of Berryman. "I heard someone say they could see it behind us," he said, collected at last. "But I wasn't able. Harry is going to try to gather some details from an officer."

"And you?" she asked. "Are you still working at this hour?"

"An extra assignment, I suppose."

"Not breaking into passenger cabins again, are you?"

"No, no, of course not."

He should have kept talking. In his mind a hundred topics fought to be voiced, but he waited too long, and she said nothing either, and after a moment they both faced a massive, impenetrable silence.

Nervously Patrick stepped back, and she held out one of her

small, thin hands. It hung there, waiting for him to do something. He stared at it blankly. The world around them went silent. There was no *Titanic*, no endless sea, no dark night sky. Only the two of them on that deck.

And then, thank God, two older first-class boys stepped between them. One of the boys—Jack, if Patrick remembered correctly—turned back and said, "Take her hand, you dolt!"

Immediately Patrick extended his cold and shaking hand. Emily pressed it briefly, smiled, and continued on her way.

The cold air ripped through his thin jacket, but he felt as warm as if he'd been standing beside one of the boilers. He found himself smiling, too, and clenched his teeth to stifle the grin. This was a time to be serious. Harry would be expecting him before too long.

Despite the late hour, men and women were stepping out of their cabins, moving toward the promenades, asking for details. Why had the engine stopped? What was that strange noise, that feeling of the ship shifting its position? Had *Titanic* collided with another boat? Patrick had no answers and no time to wonder with them.

Harry had asked Patrick to put the book in a safe place, and to him, that meant the hands of his brother, whether James was sick or not. So he hurried off to the infirmary.

When he arrived, a nurse approached, strapping on a strange vest. "Get your life belt," she said.

His life belt? He didn't even know if he had one. "Why?" he asked.

"They're talking about loading the boats. A precaution, I'm sure, but all the same . . ."

Patrick looked into the empty room behind her. "Where are your patients?"

"There are none."

"What about my brother? James Waters?"

"He went back down into the boiler rooms no more than ten minutes ago. A brave man, that one. When the engines stopped he shot right up. He said something was wrong, that they'd need his help. Now, if you'll excuse me," she finished, and stepped around him, hustling to the stairs.

Down on E Deck, off-duty trimmers were rushing out of their bunks. Patrick pushed between them, recognizing no one, and made for the spiral stairs. The sound of many boots pounding on metal steps rose up from below and a dozen trimmers and firemen emerged, panting and panicking. Two were soaked through and shivering, and several urged Patrick to turn the other way.

Patrick stopped one of the men, put a hand on his sopped shoulder. "What happened?"

"She's got a gash in her side as wide as a building and she's swallowing water through the bow."

"I have to get to the boiler rooms," Patrick said.

"You won't be getting there this way," the man said. "The

firemen's passage is flooded and they've closed the watertight doors leading astern. I'm not sure she has much time."

"The ship, you mean?" Patrick asked. "That can't be right. *Titanic* is unsinkable."

"She *was*."

Patrick sprinted back across the length of the boat. He figured he'd get to James through the engine room, but when he finally did make it down there, the way was blocked.

He cursed himself. The watertight doors! He didn't quite understand what that trimmer had been talking about when he said they'd closed the doors, but now it was clear. These were the doors he'd slipped through to walk from one boiler room to the next. Now, with the doors sealed, each boiler room was sealed off, too.

There had to be another way to reach his brother; an emergency route of some sort. They'd thought of everything in designing this ship, hadn't they? He scanned the room for a familiar face, someone to ask. Chief Engineer Bell was there, but he was talking with the distinguished, white-bearded Captain Smith and several others Patrick recognized from the Smoking Room. Patrick tried to get Bell's attention, but one of the other men waved him away. "This is important business!" the man said.

Patrick turned and rushed back up to E Deck.

There, a moment later on Scotland Road, he saw a trimmer emerge from a door on the starboard side of the busy hall. The man's overalls were soaked below the knee.

Patrick caught him and grabbed him by the straps of his overalls. "James Waters," he said, "have you seen him?"

"Sure have," the man replied. "He'd be below us, down the fidley ladder," he said, pointing back to the door. "But I wouldn't head down if I were you. The water's rising fast."

Patrick ignored the warning, slipped through the door and found an emergency ladder leading straight down to the belly of the boat. The steel ladder was cold and wet; his hands soon tired but he dared not look down. A fall would kill him.

He reached a catwalk above the boiler room floor and found James working alongside Blaney, beside a bunker on the port side. The color had not returned to his brother's face, nor the strength to his arms. Physically, he was a blurred reflection of himself.

James stopped when he saw Patrick. His expression was blank, emotionless. Then he shook his head and laughed. He dropped his shovel, raced to his brother and wrapped him in a bone-crushing hug.

James pulled the felt-wrapped *Essaies* from his waistline. "You're here for this?"

Patrick took the sweat-soaked package. Harry would be happy to have it back, of course, but he'd be mortified to see it so drenched in perspiration.

"Tell me, what has my little brother gotten himself into now?"

"It's nothing, I—"

"Blaney and Dickson were telling me a man was down here after you. They said he called you a thief. But that's not right, is it?"

Ashamed that he had even considered stealing the book, Patrick answered no.

"What's this one then?" he asked, pointing at the book.

"It's a long, long story."

"Too difficult for your laborer brother to follow?" James joked.

A trimmer raced past, heading the way Patrick had come, and yelled for James to join him. "We have to get out of here!"

Over the hissing boilers James shouted back, "Go on, I'm staying." The effort required to raise his voice produced another coughing fit—he stifled it by slapping himself on the chest, as if he were beating a drum. "You go with him, Patrick. Get yourself in a boat."

"But the lifeboats are only a precaution."

James shook his head. "That's what they'll tell the passengers. I'm telling *you* it's a necessity. *Titanic* may not last the night—not with the way the water's rushing in at the bow."

"But . . ."

Until then, until he heard it from his brother, Patrick hadn't really considered that *Titanic* might sink. She was too grand! How could a single iceberg damage her? They were surrounded by a reinforced, impenetrable structure of iron and steel, welded and riveted together by the finest shipbuilders in the world!

"Go, Patrick! Please."

"I'm not leaving without you."

"Patrick, I have to stay. As long as her lights are on, there's a chance another ship could see us. *Titanic* needs power, Patrick."

"I'm staying by your side," Patrick said. "Don't keep us both down here. Come with me, please."

James closed his eyes and ran a hand through his hair. Finally he hustled over and said something to Blaney, then strode past Patrick, heading to the catwalk, before turning back and shouting, "So, are you coming then? We'll go have ourselves a breath of fresh air."

NO INTEREST IN ICEBERGS

To think that he trusted them! Only for a few moments, to be sure, but he was supremely disappointed in himself nonetheless. Berryman had left Rockwell in the Smoking Room, awaiting his cognac, and announced convincingly that he was off in search of more information about this supposed collision.

But of course he had no interest in icebergs. All the confused, sleepwalking passengers trading falsehoods about the state of the ship annoyed him thoroughly. The world was dominated by ignorance! Next to what they were about to uncover in the *Essaies*, this little event with the iceberg was laughably inconsequential. Yet what Berryman realized, mere moments after he had hurried off to marshal his thoughts, was that he was at a supreme disadvantage.

Rockwell had the key to the cipher.

Harry owned the book.

Berryman had nothing but an agreement.

There was no cause to stop them from dispensing with him. Nothing but their word, and he knew that a promise from Rockwell was as sturdy as a sapling. He could lift the key to the cipher off Rockwell any time. That would be easy. What he needed, if he was to ensure that he had equal access to the power of alchemy, was to be in control of the book itself.

Near the end of the Promenade Deck he saw the young lady who'd been with the boy after he broke into their cabin. As Berryman passed her she studied him closely. To obscure her view, he lifted a hand to his face as if he were rubbing his cheek.

Berryman wore no disguise, so he doubted severely that she would be able to recognize him, but he hurried away nonetheless. He needed to find the boy. From Harry's offhand statement—"he will get proper care"—Berryman naturally deduced that Patrick had entrusted the volume to a friend. Clearly this friend was suffering through some illness or injury. Why else would Harry feel it necessary to make that point? Furthermore, Harry's precise choice of words—"*proper* care"— suggested that he was not receiving the best treatment possible. Therefore, he would not be in the passenger hospital. He would be in the slightly less advanced crew facilities.

His shoulder was throbbing powerfully; Berryman himself needed proper care. The makeshift sling he'd fashioned was hardly keeping his arm immobile. He descended the stairs gently.

A nurse passed him, on her way up, and he reached back and stopped her. "Are you from the crew hospital?" he asked.

"I am."

"Your patients, where are they?"

She hesitated, suspicious.

"I am a doctor and a friend of Captain Smith," he lied. "He asked me to ensure that they are safe."

"We're all clear. We had only one patient, a trimmer, and he returned to the furnaces."

"Wonderful, wonderful," Berryman replied, and continued on his way.

Of course! The boy was friends with those coal-stained brutes. That's why he ran to them. That's why they protected him.

This sequence of deductions and its logical end invigorated Berryman. He forgot the pain in his shoulder and quickened his steps. The Waters boy and his coal-stained conspirator wouldn't stay down there long. That much he could guess. But how would he intercept them? And where?

Mr. Berryman stopped at the aft end of Scotland Road. Passengers, seamen, cooks, and stewards were crowding the hall, moving fore and aft. They were calm, but hurried, and entirely too distracting for a man who needed to think. Mr. Berryman backed into an unmarked doorway and granted himself a moment to consider his next move.

A NOBLE CALLING

As they climbed the ladder, Patrick could feel the boat listing to one side and pitching forward. He imagined *Titanic*'s bold bow leaning forward at an angle now, instead of standing up straight, as if the boat herself were genuflecting before the dark ocean.

James was above him. They stopped at a landing on F Deck to rest, and while the circumstances were hardly what he had envisioned, Patrick was thrilled to be with his brother.

He would introduce him to Harry; perhaps they'd all climb aboard one of the lifeboats together. True, the two men could not have been more different. One worked with fire, the other with ink. What would they talk about? Patrick pictured them sitting across from one another in one of the lifeboats, their faces blank, and he nearly laughed.

"You're clutching that book like it's an infant," James said. "It's special?"

Patrick began reciting Harry's thoughts on the value of rare books, then stopped himself. None of that would mean anything to James.

Yet his brother did grasp the essential point.

"So it's worth a great deal of money?"

"Exactly."

"That's reason enough to be careful. So what is it about?"

"The book? Well, it's philosophical. You wouldn't like it."

"Really?" James responded, eyebrows raised.

"I don't mean . . . what I meant is that I don't think it's the kind of thing . . . it's useless, really." Patrick said this, but no longer believed it. "Why are you laughing?"

James's laugh quickly transitioned to a cough. He spat out a few drops of blood, which fell through the grates at their feet to the decks below. It truly was a long way down.

The coughing failed to diminish his smile. After a series of slow, successful breaths James said, "We both know I'm not an intellectual, Patrick, but I hardly believe books are useless. I want to know what you think of the book, not what you think I want to hear."

"But you despise books, given what happened to Dad—"

"No, Patrick, you're wrong. It wasn't the words with Dad, no matter what our dear mother says. He had faults, but reading was not one of them. He was a good man, Patrick. He had a sharp mind. I don't have that mind, Patrick. I was born with a strong back instead." James breathed in through his nose. "But you and I are different, Patrick. You shouldn't be ashamed to use that mind of yours." He tapped him on the back. "We both know you're not meant for the boiler room, so if you can do something with books, you should. It's a noble calling so long as you dedicate yourself to it honestly."

Patrick clutched the book closer. He had resisted at first, reasoning that it would be too much to explain, but now he had to tell James about the deal. One hundred pounds! His brother would be impressed. No, he'd be amazed!

Before he could go on, though, James resumed climbing. When they reached E Deck, Patrick called up to him. "I came in through that door there," he said.

James waited for him to step off onto the platform, then opened the door to the hall. A man jumped out of the way, surprised. Then he turned.

Without a word, Berryman leaped at Patrick, drove him to the platform floor.

James immediately pulled him off Patrick, but Berryman sprang up and drove his shoulder into James's stomach. A small shower of blood erupted from James's mouth.

But Patrick's brother was undeterred. He hurled their assailant against the steel ladder. Berryman lost his footing and then grabbed hold of the ladder. He wailed, hanging on with one arm as the other dangled limply at his side.

Out in the hall, Patrick heard Emily yelling, "Through there!"

A half-dozen men were with her, including a particularly angry seaman with a bandaged nose. Berryman eyed the approaching crew and began climbing immediately, steadying himself with his one good arm. He was up a flight before the men followed, scampering after him.

James tried to join in the pursuit, but Patrick held his brother back. "Let him go," he said. "We need to stay together."

HELP WILL COME

By the time Patrick, Emily, and James reached the Boat Deck, *Titanic* was listing sharp to starboard. Hurrying through the ship's halls was like crossing the side of a hill. When they did get outside, the deck was far more crowded than before. They had to slow to a walk and edge their way through the milling passengers, the vast majority of whom were strapped into cork-lined life belts.

The sense of alarm had not yet spread from the boiler rooms. Patrick found the mood to be eerily calm. Some of the men sipped drinks, others smoked cigars; a few appeared to be sleepwalking. Patrick recognized several ladies from the Reading & Writing Room; they were approaching the whole affair as leisurely as they would an afternoon tea.

The man who managed the gymnasium was inviting people

to try the exercise equipment inside. "A few turns on the bicycle will warm you right up!" he said. Patrick also thought he heard the orchestra playing, but it must have been his imagination.

The officers and crew kept the order, permitting only women and children into the lifeboats. One or two had already been dispatched.

The lights blinked, then brightened, and James began wringing his hands.

"What is it?" Patrick asked.

"We need to get you two in a boat."

"You mean the three of us," Patrick said.

James looked away. "Yes, right. Where's your mum?" he asked, turning to Emily. "Is she in a boat already?"

"No, she wouldn't get in without me," Emily answered.

Through the crowd Patrick saw Emily's complicated, colorful hat. Her mother was holding it at her side. "Mrs. Walsh! Mrs. Walsh!"

She pushed through several huddled men, grabbed Emily's hands. "Not a good time to run off, my dear!"

Handing her daughter her precious hat, she turned to Patrick. "Thank you, Mr. Waters."

A seaman took Mrs. Walsh's elbow, pointing over the rail. "Two seats for you here. No delay now, please."

"Be careful!" Emily urged before going over the rail.

"Yes," he began, but she was gone, into the boat, before he could finish.

"Now let's find you a spot," James said.

"You mean us."

"Yes, right," James said.

Patrick held out the book. "First I should bring this to Harry. He'll be down one deck, in the Smoking Room."

On A Deck, through one of the stained glass windows, Patrick saw several dozen men reclining in the Smoking Room, playing cards and conversing, wearing life belts over their dinner jackets.

"At their leisure, aren't they?" James said. "If this weren't a sinking ship, I'd say that's the place for me."

Mr. Rockwell remained in his seat, sniffing cognac in a spherical crystal glass. He was thoroughly relaxed, with his feet resting on the table before him and his jacket cast over the back of an adjacent chair. Harry stood a few tables away, sipping coffee and observing the action outside.

He hurried over when the brothers entered.

"Patrick! We thought you'd disappeared. This is your brother?"

The two men shook, but Rockwell, cognac in hand, interrupted before Patrick could introduce them properly. He was staring wide-eyed at the *Essaies*.

"You have my book . . . I mean Harry's book?"

"Yes," Patrick said, and handed the volume to Harry.

"Now," Rockwell said to Harry, "may I see it?"

"Where is Berryman?" Harry asked.

Rockwell flicked his hand in the air. "Inconsequential."

James pulled at Patrick's coat. "Listen, Patrick, I—"

The boat shifted, listing to port. Drinks slid on the tables, stopping at the raised edges, and Harry's coffee spilled over the rim of his cup, staining the white cuff of his dress shirt. He winced and set down the cup.

"I'm beginning to believe that the resolution of our little mystery should be postponed," Harry declared. "We should all be moving to the boats."

Mr. Rockwell reached out to grab the volume.

"Archibald, honestly!" Harry said. "We can unlock the text later."

"No, Harry, I must have that book. I've waited too long."

He lunged forward, and Patrick kicked at one of his small feet. Mr. Rockwell toppled, and the two stewards from earlier hurried over.

"Keep him from bothering us," Harry told them.

As Rockwell shouted in protest, Harry motioned for James and Patrick to follow him out. On the deck, they were quickly swallowed by a sea of passengers, and struggled to stay together.

"I need to find my parents," Harry called over his shoulder.

"We'll come with you," Patrick answered.

James did not seem keen to go searching, but he followed them up to the Boat Deck nevertheless. Once again the lights flickered. Inside the Marconi Room, Bride and Philips were hurriedly knocking out messages.

Patrick leaned through the doorway. "The ship is in trouble. You should find a spot in a boat!"

Bride waved him off. "We're signaling anyone who's listening, hoping someone will steam to our rescue. As long as the Marconi is working, there's hope," he said. Then he looked at James bitterly. "God bless the men in the engine rooms for maintaining the power."

James backed away and stared out at the dark water. His jaw was set and he was clenching his fists.

"James, he didn't mean—"

"He was right to say it, Patrick."

James turned back, laid his hands on Patrick's shoulders, and stared at him with unexpected calm. "I shouldn't be here, Patrick. You heard the man. *Titanic* needs power. She needs her trimmers and firemen down in the boiler rooms, not up here looking for a way to escape. I need to get back to where I belong," he said, "and you need to get yourself in a boat."

"Please," Patrick began, but he stopped himself. There was no use. He could see that his brother was set. James was wringing his hands, burning to return to the boilers.

Patrick stared down at his now scuffed shoes. How long had

they been together? Twenty minutes? Thirty? Now they were about to part ways again. He didn't know what to say.

James shook Patrick by the shoulders and smiled. "Don't worry yourself! I'll get out before she goes down. But I can't take care of the both of us down there." James coughed, then squeezed Patrick's thin shoulders and leaned in close, lowering his voice. "Promise me you'll find a seat, brother."

Patrick nodded. "I will, but you have to promise me—"

"I'll be grand, Patrick," James said. "Help will come."

31

NO GOODBYES

H arry cursed as they angled through the crowd. "I don't see them," he said.

Patrick had no reply; his thoughts were with James.

"There!" Harry shouted.

Several officers were urging women and children into a lifeboat. Mr. Widener stood at the edge of the cluster of people, arguing with his wife.

"Mother! Father!" Harry called.

His mother saw him first and waved with great relief. She had the same large brow as Harry, her eyes set in the same dark shadows. "Harry, dear, where have you been?"

Harry held out the book. "The little Bacon, mother. I had to retrieve it."

"Of course you did," she said.

"Thank goodness you're here now," Mr. Widener said. "She wouldn't board until she saw you. Would you please tell your dear mother that we will be perfectly fine?"

"He is right, mother. There are other boats, and we'll join you shortly if you're not back up here on deck in an hour."

After a brief embrace with husband and son, Mrs. Widener stepped up and over the rail, holding an officer's hand, and took the appointed seat.

The crew was preparing to lower the boat into the sea when Mrs. Widener spotted Patrick as if for the first time. Her expression changed. She called to the officer. "Wait! What about the boy?"

"Too old," the officer replied. "Boys of more than ten years are men."

The boat, suspended by ropes from great iron cranes, began to descend. Mrs. Widener's eyes turned red. Harry started to say something, but his father added under his breath, "No goodbyes, son. No goodbyes."

After the boat had dropped out of sight, Harry turned to his father. "What do you suggest we do now?"

"For now we wait, like gentlemen," Mr. Widener said. "I propose the Smoking Room."

Harry nodded in agreement, and they started toward the stairs. Patrick did not understand it; the two men seemed almost leisurely. "Harry," he said, half-whispering, "shouldn't we wait for a boat?"

"We will, Patrick," Harry answered. "Let them attend to the women and children first. There is time."

Patrick followed them down and into the Smoking Room, but before the door had closed behind them, Mr. Widener turned back, declaring that they should make one more trip to their staterooms. Patrick was growing impatient. Surely there had to be room in the boats now. He stopped.

"Stay with us, Patrick," Harry said. Then he tilted his head, spotting something over Patrick's shoulder.

Patrick turned to look. Harry was staring at an empty table; the same place they'd sat with Rockwell. Then he saw it on the rug, behind one of the chairs: a rectangular strip of paper. The key to the cipher. It must have fallen out of Rockwell's coat.

"Is that it?" Patrick asked.

"We do have more pressing concerns," Harry said, "and we could certainly wait until we're ashore to look up the key ourselves. But I confess that I am quite curious."

"Harry?" Mr. Widener called from the doorway.

"One moment," Harry said. "Go ahead, Patrick."

Patrick raced over, picked up the thick rectangular strip, then handed it to his tutor as they followed Mr. Widener to the stairs.

Holding the paper aloft, Harry said, "He'll thank us! I'm a man of my word, Patrick . . . I will hold to our agreement."

There was a note of uncertainty in his voice. "But?"

"But I do think we'd both benefit from a mental diversion at the moment," Harry said. They turned at the bottom of the steps to descend another flight. "So what say we decipher this message tonight?"

Patrick smiled. "I think that's a wonderful idea."

At the base of the stairs on C Deck, they turned right, past the barber's shop, toward the Wideners' rooms. The ship was tilting even more. It felt like they were walking uphill, and Patrick held one hand out against the wall as they went.

Holding the book out before him, Harry read the inscription aloud.

> Louing and beloued brother,
> Riches are for spending, and fpending
> for honour & good actions.
>   F Bacon

They reached the stateroom; Patrick waited in the doorway as the two men gathered a few final items. Harry grabbed two books—Patrick couldn't see the titles—then began translating each letter in Bacon's note into an A or a B, depending on whether it was written normally, in block-style print, or in that fancily flowing cursive. He read slowly, in groups of five. "A . . . B . . . A . . . A . . . B."

Dazed, Patrick consulted the key. The words were shaking on the page. He couldn't focus.

"Patrick? A, B, A, A, B. What does the sequence correspond to on the key?"

"Yes, yes, sorry," he said, and scanned the column again. The sequence was nearly halfway down. "K."

Harry resumed immediately. "A . . . B . . . B . . . A . . . A."

"N," Patrick responded.

Harry grabbed him by the lapels. "Ha! You said *n*? *K* and then *n*? Let me see that," he said, and he took Rockwell's handwritten key. In the doorway he held the book and the key side by side, his eyes flicking from one to the other and back. "Of course!"

For a moment Patrick forgot about the madness around them. "What is it? A formula?"

Harry's eyebrows rose up. He carefully placed the book back in its case, sliding the cipher in alongside. "What sort of tutor would I be if I gave you the answer, Patrick?"

"What do you mean?"

As Mr. Widener emerged with two glasses, two cigars, and a bottle of what Patrick guessed was very fine whiskey, Harry removed two extra life belts. "I will leave the pleasure of this discovery to you, Patrick. You'll have to crack this cipher yourself."

"Really, Harry, can't you tell me?"

Mr. Widener eyed the *Essaies* with an odd smile. "My son and his books," he said.

"What's wrong with my love of books?" Harry burst back.

"Nothing, Son, I meant—"

"I work, don't I? I toil in that mercantile building. Perhaps I'm no Morgan, but I do my best at a position for which I have no natural interest, and I resent—"

"Harry—"

"No, Father, let me finish."

Mr. Widener's voice rose nearly to a shout. "No, Harry, I won't. You misunderstand me completely, and I fear that you have for some time. I don't disapprove of your passion for books. It's beyond me, as I've said before, but I don't disapprove. In fact, I admire you. I've never loved my own work as much as you love building that collection of yours."

"But . . ."

Mr. Widener handed his son a cigar and a glass. "I couldn't be more proud of you, son. Now get your coat, and something for our young friend here as well. It's going to be a cold, cold night."

UNTIL MORNING AT LEAST

Up on the Boat Deck they waited patiently for what seemed like an hour. Most of the lifeboats had been deployed, filled only with women, small children, and the crew to row them. Patrick could see the boats scattered in the distance, faintly illuminated by the ship's lights and the countless bright stars. The thin crescent moon was not far above the horizon, and the boats were drifting farther away.

Yet Harry and his father remained optimistic: There was talk of ocean liners steaming to their rescue. Several passengers even pointed to a distant light on the horizon, insisting that it was a fast approaching ship.

Most argued that they had ample time, too. Patrick heard one man reason that even if *Titanic* were to sink, she would not do so quickly. They had until morning at least, by which point a fleet of ships would arrive.

Harry encouraged Patrick to make good use of the time and work out Bacon's message. He sat against the wall and held the book and the key to the cipher on his lap, but he was too distracted, too cold to think clearly. His hands were shaking so violently that he could hardly hold his pen.

He continued to plead for the answer, but Harry refused. "You will have plenty of time to work it out tomorrow, on the deck of our rescuer."

Patrick handed Harry the book and stood. Harry tucked it inside his coat, then removed the key to the cipher. "You keep this," he said, "and I'll hold onto the *Essaies*."

The Widener men calmly sipped their whiskeys and drew on their cigars, but Patrick had nothing to occupy him. He could sit still no longer. "Should we check the boats on the other side?" he pressed.

As the Wideners calmly considered his question, the young man who'd caught Patrick with Emily earlier that night raced past with his friend. He stopped and turned back. "Mr. Widener, have you seen my father?"

"I haven't, Jack."

"Thank you, Mr. Widener," he said. Then he lowered his voice. "Have you heard? There aren't enough boats. There's still space in the ones that have already been dropped in, though.

I'm planning to swim for one of those." He looked at the Wideners, then Patrick. "You're welcome to come with us."

The Wideners declined, Patrick hesitated, and Jack was gone.

"Do you think he is right?" Harry asked his father.

"I doubt it, Harry." Mr. Widener pointed to a spot on the deck
near the base of the third funnel, where a collection of men
stood stoically. "Ah, there he is!"

"Who?" Patrick asked.

"The lad's father, John Thayer. Wait here, I'll be back in a
moment."

The group in question looked very much above it all, watching the scene as if it were a sporting match. Patrick guessed that
Mr. Widener, back straight and cigar alight, intended to join them
in their refusal to show fear or panic, and, if necessary, go down
with the ship as a gentleman.

But Patrick was not ready to give in. "Harry," he said, "There
has to be another boat."

A new crowd broke through onto the deck. Patrick and Harry
were jammed up against the windows of the gymnasium. Two figures pushed through the throng and stopped to face them: a wild-
eyed Mr. Rockwell and a battered Berryman, his face bruised, his
whole body listing to one side.

HIS GREAT TREASURE

Apparently some strength remained in Berryman's broken body: He leaped forward and tackled Harry to the pine floor. "Give it to me!" he yelled.

Patrick kicked at Berryman's bad shoulder but missed.

Using his immense stomach like a battering ram, Mr. Rockwell bounced Patrick against the steel wall. No punch of his brother's had ever hurt so much.

Then Mr. Rockwell dropped to his knees beside Harry and Berryman, trying to wrestle away the book. But Harry clutched it to his chest with both arms.

Out of the crowd came Mr. Webb. He grabbed Berryman around the midsection, hoisted him up into the air, and squeezed. Mr. Webb's face was bright red with exertion and Berryman's turned a breathless, pained purple. In all the clamor, Patrick detected the deep snap of bones breaking in two.

Mr. Webb dropped him, and Berryman crumpled into a formless heap, able to breathe but not to move. Next Mr. Webb turned to Rockwell. "We are *trying* to maintain order," he said.

Thoroughly intimidated, Mr. Rockwell backed away. "You'll see to it that the *Essaies* survive, won't you Harry? You won't be so foolish as to let the book drown?"

"The book will survive the night," Harry insisted.

"Then I believe I'll test the water," Rockwell said, and he promptly rolled himself over the rail, into the frigid sea.

The splash was closer than Patrick expected. Just a few hours earlier the Boat Deck loomed several stories above the surface of the ocean. Now the sea was rising ever higher, the ship sinking lower; Mr. Rockwell hadn't fallen far.

Mr. Webb peered over the rail and nodded.

"Thank you, Mr. Webb," Patrick said.

"Of course, Mr. Waters. It was a pleasure to work together." He placed his hands on Patrick's shoulders. "No more spittoons for you, Patrick. Please do your best to survive."

Before Patrick could reply, Mr. Webb walked back into the crowd, urging people to remain calm.

Berryman's body was as formless as a wet shirt thrown to the floor, but he could not give in. "I can see it, Harry. I can see that you know. Please, I beg you, do me the courtesy of telling me what you found. I worked so hard. You don't understand . . ."

"It's over," Patrick said. "It's all over."

His face white from the pain, Berryman said, "But the formula . . . you must tell me . . ."

Harry kneeled beside his old classmate and whispered into his ear.

Berryman's pale, pained face plainly displayed his confusion. His expression changed from openmouthed horror to disbelief, then it slowly relaxed into a resigned, small happiness. "Yes," he said at last. "That would be his great treasure, wouldn't it?"

THE LAST OF THE LIFEBOATS

Distress rockets exploded above them; the brilliant white bursts of light looked like falling stars. Patrick thought he heard gunshots. The band—he had not imagined the music after all—continued with the soothing, classical tunes better suited to one of *Titanic*'s long and leisurely first-class dinners, the gymnasium's instructor was still selling people on the virtues of his exercise bicycles, and the ship's deck and cabin lights blinked occasionally but continued glowing brightly, creating a silver sheen on the water nearby. The lights meant she still had power, and that Patrick's friends Bride and Philips were still able to tap out distress signals. James was doing his job.

Yet no rescue ships were in sight. That bright light near the horizon had been an illusion; if it was a ship, then she had fled the scene. Patrick felt a chill in his chest and stomach as he looked out at the boats in the distance: He and Harry might have to swim for one of them after all.

For now, though, they sought an easier way to survive. The final lifeboat had been lowered to A Deck, as the Boat Deck had become too crowded, and Patrick insisted that they try for a spot.

First Harry stood on his toes, studying the crowd. "I don't see him. He said to wait here."

Patrick thought he recognized the back of Mr. Widener's head at the top of the stairs to A Deck. "Is that him?"

The man was out of view before Harry could confirm it was his father. "I couldn't tell. Let's go and have a look."

Downstairs, a thick crowd pushed toward the boat, which was hanging suspended outside the glass, only partially full. Patrick peered through one of the open windows. The cold black water, oily at the surface, was only two body lengths below. He could hear the water rushing and roiling through the flooded lower decks. James was in one of the rear boiler rooms, he reminded himself. The rear rooms would be the last to flood.

Soon enough, though, the water would be flooding over the windows, pouring onto the very deck on which he stood. He studied the horizon again, but saw nothing to buoy his hope.

"I don't see him," Harry said.

In the crowd ahead Patrick spotted the man he'd believed to be Mr. Widener. He had been mistaken. "I'm sorry," he said.

Harry glanced back toward the stairs, then suggested they push ahead. They did not get far. The officers had formed a human fence. One of them stopped a boy about Patrick's age from passing through until his father protested and they let him go.

"Women and children ONLY," the officer shouted afterward. "No more boys!"

In response, a first-class woman pushing closer to the boat removed her hat and squashed it down on her son's head, wrapped her woolen shawl around his shoulders. Patrick heard her urge him quietly: "Keep your head down and don't say a word."

Her trick worked, and they both climbed in, but there were no more overt exceptions to the rule. Patrick watched as an elegant, upright man—Mr. Webb had told him he was one of the wealthiest people in the world—walked away from the boat and back toward the stairs, his face all gloom and darkness.

"Mrs. Astor is on that boat," Harry said, pointing to a woman no older than James, and seated near the middle. "If they're not letting the Colonel aboard, I have no hope of winning a seat. You should try, though, Patrick. They might be lenient."

He stared at the boy in his mother's frilly, flowered hat and feminine shawl, seated comfortably in the boat. He couldn't do that and he couldn't leave Harry. There had to be another way. "No," Patrick insisted, "let's get back up to the Boat Deck. We'll stay dry and warm as long as we can and then swim for one of the other boats."

Many of those departed lifeboats did have room; Jack Thayer was right about that. The problem was that they were also moving farther and farther away. If he and Harry were to make one of those boats, they would have to go soon. Patrick proposed the plan.

A sad smile formed on Harry's pale face. "I can't swim," he admitted.

Patrick slapped his tutor's life belt. "This will float you high enough," he said, "and I'll help you move."

Harry looked dazed, as if his mind was elsewhere; he pressed a hand to his side.

"Are you hurt?" Patrick asked.

Harry snapped back to the moment. "Hurt? No. And your plan . . . it is perfect. We'll do exactly that, Patrick."

Up on the Boat Deck, a large group of passengers and crew was struggling to release one of the collapsible boats from the top of the officers' quarters. They were jamming oars beneath the boat, working to wedge it loose.

"That could hold us," Patrick said.

"Not all of us."

Harry was right: Countless men were staring hopefully at the boat. It could hold forty or fifty, Patrick guessed, but at least twice that number stood waiting, and there were masses more spread out around the deck and huddled inside, out of the cold. Harry was hurriedly writing something on a piece of his stationary. He folded it over several times and slipped it inside the felt cover, with the Bacon.

"You said you're a strong swimmer, Patrick?"

"Yes. We'll be fine, Harry. We'll make it to one of those other boats."

Harry began to remove his life belt.

"No, Harry, you'll need that—"

The men up above were cursing and calling for a knife. The ropes securing the boat weren't coming loose.

"Don't be alarmed, I'll put it back on," Harry said. Then he took off his coat and handed it to Patrick. "Wear this to stay warm, and then fasten your life belt over it."

Patrick was not about to refuse. He was already freezing; any added layer of warmth would do. Once he'd buttoned the coat they both retied their belts.

"Who has a knife?" the men called out again.

Beneath the shouts, someone was calling out weakly. Patrick followed the sound and found Berryman, eyes closed, face color-less, propped against a wall.

"Is that you, Waters?" he asked.

Patrick paused before answering. The man had tried to kill him, yet it was sad seeing him so broken.

Mr. Berryman opened his eyes, removed his book knife and held it out. "This might help," he said.

Without a word Patrick took the knife and raced it to the men.

One of the officers reached down, grabbed the blade, and eyed it skeptically. Then he pressed it against a length of rope and nodded. "This will do."

More signal rockets exploded high in the air. Some crewmember or sleepy-eyed night watchman on a distant boat had to see those flares. Someone had to come save them.

The boat pitched farther forward. Harry fell over a bald, wrinkled older man smoking a cigar. Neither apologized. Panic had begun to set in; manners were no longer relevant.

The talk of rescue ships quieted. No one maintained the illusion that *Titanic* would float until dawn. They all knew it now: The ship was doomed. A trimmer burst out of a door in one of the boiler casings; he'd climbed up one of the fidley escape ladders. Patrick watched the door, hoping to see James step through, but he knew his brother would be down until the very last moment.

Patrick gripped his tutor's arm; he couldn't stand there waiting. "Let's get to the stern."

"Patrick?"

But he was already hurrying astern, weaving through passengers, annoyed by the too large coat. Now was no time to trip and fall.

"Patrick!"

He turned; Harry had not moved.

"What?" he asked, racing back. "What is it?"

A few shouts of satisfaction came from above the officer's quarters. The men had freed the boat. Now they were trying to lower it into the water.

"Be sure you swim for the nearest boat, Patrick."

"Yes, I know, that's what we said—"

"Don't stop moving. The water is cold and you'll feel a shock, but don't stop moving."

An intensely loud gurgling resounded near the front of the ship and beneath them, as if a colossal pot of water were boiling over.

"Harry, I know, but we should—"

Before he could finish a mass of white and blue water roared up the deck from the bow. Passengers and officers were swept up off their feet and washed astern. The wave struck Harry in the back, his tutor's eyes flashed wide, and then the water swallowed Patrick as well. Crowds of people were tumbling inside the whitewater. Someone kicked Patrick in the mouth, his shoulder bashed against a wall, and his hands ran across something hard as iron.

A rail! He gripped it with both hands and his feet swung up, level with his hands, as the water rushed past.

The wave was too powerful. Another moment and his hands were free again. The wave washed him back over the deck, tumbling him over the freshly stained wood, bouncing him like a weightless ball. Nothing hurt. He was too cold and frightened to feel.

Then the bouncing stopped; he felt no more of the ship. He was falling, surrounded by water, sucked into the endless depths of the cold dark ocean.

TRAPPED IN A WATERY VISE

The cold pushed straight through to his core. His heart felt frozen. Yet he kept hearing Harry urging him to move. He flailed his arms, kicked, felt nothing around him—no deck, no railings, nothing to grab. The ship was gone and he was encased in a liquid tomb of ice.

His head and chest were trapped in a watery vise, the cold squeezing them down to nothing. His eyes burned when he opened them to the blue darkness. The water was churning furiously. Every kick and every desperate pull were worthless, moving him nowhere. Swimming was useless; it was like trying to pull and kick through thin air.

There was no direction, no up or down; he was lost in the water. Patrick's ears filled up, and the cold seawater soaked his brain. He had little energy left. His will was fading, his lungs commanding him to breathe. Was this what it was like to drown? He started to believe that it might be fine to breathe. He nearly sucked in a fatal lungful of the sea when the water around him suddenly calmed.

Now his efforts actually had an effect. He pulled and kicked and moved in the direction intended: up. He was finally in control again.

A dim blue light was visible above. He felt the life belt rising up to his chin and under his armpits, pulling him up to the surface. His head and shoulders shot out of the water. The searing headache and crushing grip on his chest eased at once.

Patrick breathed, the air stinging in his throat, gasped, and breathed again. He bounced up and down several times before settling at the surface with his head and shoulders clear out of the water. Now he was up, at least, and he could see *Titanic*'s lights some distance away. How had he moved that far?

There was no one around him, but he expected them to surface soon. Where was Harry? Patrick needed to help his tutor. Surely Harry had been swept along the same underwater path. They'd been right next to each other.

But no passengers popped out of the depths. Patrick was alone. In his mind he heard Harry ordering him: "Swim!"

Not too far away, men were struggling to climb atop an iceberg or some kind of floating island of ice. He swam for them, keeping his nearly frozen head out of the water. His shoes came off as he kicked. He could not feel his feet or his hands.

As he approached his target he saw that it wasn't an iceberg at all, but an overturned lifeboat—the very one he'd seen the men free from the tops of the officer's quarters before that fateful wave struck.

From a distance he made out Jack Thayer leaning over the edge of the overturned boat, helping to drag another man up out of the water.

"Help!" Patrick yelled. "Help!"

His voice was barely audible, as his chest was constricted from the cold. Patrick swam harder, warmed by the hope that he might soon be out of that water.

Jack spotted him a few strokes away and urged him on, "Keep coming! Keep coming!"

Every pull, every swing of his arms required an incredible effort. Patrick wasn't certain he was kicking at all; it felt as if his legs had been cut off at the knees. But he was moving. He knew it now. He was nearing the boat.

When he was a mere stroke away Jack reached out and reeled Patrick in; he felt like a half-dead fish, barely able to move. Jack grabbed him under one arm, an officer took the other, and they pulled him, blue and frozen, out of the sea. Immediately he was warmer, as if he'd stepped from the top of a snow-capped mountain to a hot sandy beach.

The air that had seemed so frigid earlier that night now felt tropical. It was cold, yes, but nothing compared to that black sea.

Nearly a dozen men were huddled together atop the boat and more were coming on. Harold Bride, the wireless operator, was lying on his back, unconscious.

"She's going down," Jack said quietly.

Titanic was submerged through the middle of the boat. The water was rising over the second of her great funnels. The first had already fallen. Every setting of china, every crystal wine glass, chandelier, and decanter seemed to smash together in one terrible crescendo. Horrible crashes followed, as powerful as explosions. Someone said that it was the boilers coming loose and crashing one atop the other, down toward the bow.

The hard, high-pitched sound of wrenched steel rang across the water as she was torn apart through the middle, split nearly in half. Yet there were still passengers on deck, clinging tight. The number of them had doubled, at least. They were massed together, swarming toward the stern. Patrick shut his eyes to the horror, but that only made the cries and screams grow louder. He cursed his powerful hearing. During that unending moment he would rather have been deaf.

The lights flickered, and then blacked out.

The men in the boat watched silently as *Titanic*'s stern slowly rose in the air. She began sinking steadily, her stern rising higher off the water, as if some great sea beast were gradually pulling her down by the bow.

Soon the great propellers were up and out of the water, rising until they faced the white stars overhead. Passengers jumped and dropped into the water below, creating hundreds of small splashes. From that distance the effect was like a hard rain suddenly bombarding a glassy lake.

The screams and calls, the terrible wrenching of the steel hull, those fateful splashes all combined into a horribly frightening chorus. These were sounds that no boy or man was meant to hear. This was the music of hell.

As *Titanic* slipped down, their overturned, water-filled boat was pulled toward her. The men grabbed what they could to help paddle away, fearing that they'd be sucked under. Patrick joined the men, leaning over the edge and paddling with his blue, cramped hands. He had to look to see that his hands were actually in the water. He no longer felt the cold.

Their raft slowed. A powerful silence took hold of them— Patrick heard nothing, absolutely nothing, as the unsinkable ship quietly vanished beneath the surface. *Titanic* was gone.

Harry was gone.

James was gone.

The water swirled and boiled, but did not threaten their overturned boat. Soon the sea was completely calm, as if *Titanic* had never been there at all; as if the hundreds of soaked and freezing passengers splashing and swimming desperately to stay alive had been dropped there from the sky overhead.

More and more bodies popped up, buoyed by life belts. Some were thrashing, some swimming with purpose, others lifeless and still. There was splashing everywhere; again he thought of rain on a lake. In fact, Patrick felt removed from the scene; he was merely watching it all. He was not really there.

Patrick wanted nothing more than to close his eyes and ears and embrace this feeling that he was somewhere else, but they were taking in survivors now, and he had to help. He was the only Waters man left. He had to make his family proud.

For the next half-hour they pulled more survivors up onto the boat—officers, crew, passengers. Several trimmers survived the sinking. Men who knew James and Blaney swore that if any ship did come, they would all have those brave men who remained in the engine rooms to thank.

Before long, though, the precariously floating boat began to sink too low. The only thing more painful than seeing so many souls adrift on that black water, frozen but held afloat by their vests, was turning away the stout survivors among them, the few who endured the cold and made it alongside. But the officers refused—they could bring on no more without endangering themselves.

Patrick pressed up against the men around him but could

not stop shivering. The air was no longer so tropical; his whole body was shaking from the cold.

The lifeboats were spreading out. Their overturned raft was gradually sinking, and one of the seamen onboard said they should tie up to a lifeboat with spare room, but none were within shouting distance. The bodies were also drifting apart and away, floating like buoys loosed from their moorings, and the ornate detritus of the ocean liner was everywhere. Doors, tables ripped from the floor, and deck chairs all floated past. One of the men recalled aloud that he'd been sitting on one such chair a few hours earlier, sipping hot broth.

The mere thought of warm broth reinvigorated Patrick, and he told himself over and over that hope remained. Bride kept reassuring them that a ship called *Carpathia* was on her way. They had only to survive until daybreak.

In the cold, silent hours that passed, Patrick thought of his mother, his brother, Harry Widener, Mr. Webb, Blaney, Emily, and so many more of the friends and even the enemies he'd made on the journey. He'd been to church and would have said that he believed in God if asked, but now he really, truly prayed, for himself, his family, and every man, woman, and child who'd been on *Titanic*, even Berryman and Rockwell.

Something made him wonder what his father would have done in those final hours. John Waters would not have been the classic hero, like James, but he would have done right. He might have regaled the passengers with stories to help maintain the calm, providing words and tall tales that soothed as effectively as the musicians' notes.

Before the sun rose, as a gray-yellow light creeped through the darkness, a great ship appeared. Patrick saw it first but was too tired to point. The men lacked the strength to cheer or even smile, but they were saved. *Carpathia* had arrived. So many had perished so terribly, but they would survive.

AN UNEXPECTED MESSAGE

Cold, numb, and listless, Patrick was barely able to climb *Carpathia*'s ladder and safely reach the deck. He had little feeling in his hands and his clothes were still soaked through. The cuffs of his shirt were frozen. Bride was worse off—he had to be lifted aboard.

The deck was gloom-ridden. They were among the lucky survivors, but there was no joy, no relief, only a terrible dulling sadness. There were women everywhere, but few men. An older woman wrapped a dry blanket around Patrick and pushed a cup of something warm into his hands.

Another woman hurried him into a cabin, sat him down, stripped off his soaked life belt and coat, and gave him a blanket to wrap himself up. "Keep drinking," she urged him. "And rub your arms and shoulders."

A member of *Carpathia*'s crew joined them, but Patrick couldn't really see him or the woman. They were merely voices attached to blurred figures. A thick haze covered everything, as if he was still underwater. He sipped his drink and the liquid burned his lips and throat, igniting the first sparks of a fire inside him as it trickled down. He would be warm again soon.

"I'll have those dried in the oven if you'd like," the man said of Patrick's soaked clothes.

"No," Patrick insisted. "I'd rather keep them here."

The crewmember shrugged and left.

"You were Harry Widener's ward, weren't you?" the woman asked.

"I was."

"Wait here," she said, "I know someone who will want to meet you."

Patrick nodded, closed his eyes, wrapped himself tightly in the rough wool blanket, and pulled Harry's sopped wool coat in close beside him. He had no interest in rubbing his arms—he wanted to sleep. When he spread out the coat to dry, though, he felt something inside.

The outer pockets were empty. He checked the inside and found a large pocket sewn into the inner lining. His still shivering fingers closed around soaked felt. And something thin and rectangular inside.

The *Essaies*.

Harry knew he wouldn't survive, but he had faith in Patrick. "I know it's damaged, Harry," Patrick thought aloud, "but I saved it."

"And a wonderful job you did!"

He blinked, and the haze over his eyes disappeared. There before him stood Archibald Rockwell, looking as fresh and fit as if he'd just emerged from the Turkish Baths.

"Mr. Rockwell! But you—"

"My significant girth has its advantages, Patrick," he said. "The cold cannot penetrate this shell! I'm as fit for these waters as a seal and could have waded for another few hours at least. Thankfully I managed to tread over to one of those delightfully undermanned lifeboats. I reclined on one of its benches and slept peacefully while a dear group of ladies rowed us to safety. I've since had more than a few warming cups of chocolate and brandy, but I confess that I was feeling rather depressed until I saw you."

"Please, Mr. Rockwell. Harry wanted me to protect this book."

"And thankfully you did! I confess that when I failed to find Mr. Widener aboard this angelic vessel I was despondent. But then I heard that young Widener's ward survived and, oh, what delightful news!"

That kind woman . . . had she really betrayed him?

"You can't have it. I'll yell."

Rockwell produced a pistol. "On the contrary, Patrick. Now, the *Essaies*, please."

Patrick stared into the pistol's dark barrel. He couldn't give in now. "No."

With surprising speed Rockwell slapped him across the face with the back of his hand. Instantly Patrick's cheek was afire from the pain. The taste of hot blood filled his mouth. His eyes went black.

Another click resounded behind them. One of *Carpathia's* officers stood pointing a pistol at Mr. Rockwell's head.

Behind him waited a second officer and a woman whose eyes were the dark, shadowy image of Harry's: Mrs. Widener.

"Arrest him," she said. "He was trying to steal my son's book."

"And he did steal my pistol," the other officer added.

Mr. Rockwell dropped the gun.

"This is outrageous!" he said as one of the officers bound his hands behind his back. "I am an important man! The boy is the thief!"

"Lock him up," the first officer ordered.

As they pushed Mr. Rockwell out of the room he yelled to Patrick. "Tell me, please! Tell me what you find!"

Patrick looked again at the woman's dark eyes. He had only seen her for a moment on the Boat Deck. Now he could see that she was a near mirror image of Harry. "Thank you, Mrs. Widener."

He handed her the book.

She held it carefully. "You were with them earlier, weren't you? You were Harry's steward."

"I was."

Mrs. Widener pressed a kerchief to her face to stop herself from crying. Tears pooled in Patrick's eyes.

"He liked you, though you did vex him," she said with a smile. She held up the book. "This is his precious Bacon?"

"Yes . . . I . . ."

"Go on."

"I don't think he believed he'd survive, so he gave it to me."

"And you nearly sacrificed your life instead of giving it to that criminal oaf . . . Harry truly did have an influence on you."

"Yes, Mrs. Widener, he did."

She ran her fingers over the cover, then handed the book back to Patrick. "He'd want you to have it then."

"No, I couldn't—"

"Take it," she said, pressing the kerchief to her eyes. Through tears she added, "Stay here, I'll see about getting you something else to drink."

She left, and Patrick opened to the inscription. A piece of Harry's stationery, folded over several times, fell to the floor. On it he'd written a brief note:

> Patrick,
> Never mind Livesey and Gunn. Jim
> was the hero. Without him that
> treasure would have been lost forever.

Be the hero of your own story, Patrick,
and follow Bacon's secret.

Yours,

Harry

From his pocket he removed the sodden key to the cipher. The letters were smudged but legible. He laid it flat on the opposite page.

A group of women passed the doorway. One turned back.

"You're alive!" Emily yelled.

She ran forward and embraced him before he could stand, then backed away.

"Barely," he said.

Her mother called to her from down the hall.

"One moment, Mother. I'll meet you at the cabin."

"Your hat?" Patrick asked.

"Gone. I'd like to think the birds flew it to safety."

She smiled, and Patrick decided he would buy her a new one someday. One with even more birds.

Emily looked down at the book and the rectangular paper. "Is that it?" she asked, excited. "What does it say?"

"We're about to find out. Here, you can help," Patrick said, handing her the key.

They sat side by side, with a comfortable space between them, against the wall. He was shivering again, but it did not bother him.

"What do I do?"

"It's fairly simple. I'll read a sequence of As and Bs. You find the matching sequence on the key, and read me the letter."

Briefly she studied the paper. "Good. Go ahead."

"A, B, A, A, B," he said.

"K."

"A, B, B, A, A."

"That would be an *n*."

"And now, A, B, B, then an A and another B."

"Let me see . . . *p*? No, that's not right. You said B, A, B at the end? That would be *o*."

"How about B, A, B, and then two As?"

"W."

"Interesting . . . but I doubt . . ."

"What?"

"Nothing. Let's go on. A, B, A, B, A."

"L."

Patrick nearly leaped to his feet. "You said k, n, o, w, l, right?"

"Yes," Emily said. "That's right."

"Ha! Of course. That's why Berryman laughed!"

He took the key and examined the next few letters.

"What do you mean?" Emily pressed. "What are you talking about?"

"Sir Francis Bacon's great secret wasn't a formula, and it wasn't a map to some great treasure. It was a statement! A single, powerful statement."

"What was it?" she asked.

Patrick closed the book, stared at the slowly drying old paper, the slightly worn edges. "The one collection of words that summarizes all his philosophy."

"Yes?"

"For a man like Bacon, or Harry, for that matter, it is the key to unlimited wealth."

"So what is it?" Emily pressed.

"Knowledge is power," Patrick said. He smiled, thinking of his tutor. "Knowledge is power."

EPILOGUE

Harvard College, May 1922

On a warm morning in May, Patrick Waters led his mother across the green of Harvard Yard, under the shelter of wide-leafed oaks. He pointed at each of the many brick-faced buildings along the way, how'd he'd lived for a time in that hall, studied in another. But in truth he had little passion for any of these structures. Above all else, he wanted his mother to see the library.

She had arrived only the day before, and she took in the campus with the wonder of a child. "I still don't see why you had to study here when we have a fine university in Belfast . . ."

"But?"

She took his arm and smiled. "But it is a beautiful school now, isn't it?"

In the middle of another stretch of grass she turned to the

north and frowned at the sight of the understated Memorial Church. "Very simple for a place of worship."

Patrick took his mother by the shoulders and turned her around to face the massive, powerful library to the south. He regarded the building as nothing less than a temple, a church of learning and knowledge. The powerful columns, the noble façade, the perfectly aligned, wide stone steps that invited passing students to enter and read, and the sense of permanence that the building conveyed—it looked as if the library had been crafted from a single, massive boulder.

His mother read the name carved in tall, scripted letters into the gray stone above the columns. "The Harry Elkins Widener Memorial Library . . . is that the man from the ship?"

Patrick nodded with a sad smile. The ship. Ten years later, she still couldn't pronounce the name *Titanic* aloud. She stared at the library for some time without saying a word. He knew she was thinking of James.

Now Patrick took her arm. "If I had the money, I'd build him an even grander monument," Patrick said.

His mother looked at him curiously, then shook her head. Her eyes shone from slight tears. "I wasn't thinking of James. I was thinking of your father and how he would have loved this. He would have been so proud of you, our professor."

"I'm hardly a professor yet, Mother. Now, should we go inside?"

"I would be delighted."

As they climbed the steps and passed through the doors, Patrick removed a felt-wrapped book from his coat pocket. He asked his mother to wait for a moment, and walked to a young librarian seated at a wide desk against the wall. After carefully removing the green felt, he laid a frail, small book on the desk. He'd held on to it in the decade since the ship sank, even through the four years he had been studying at Harvard College. But now, with his graduation approaching, the time had come.

"Returning?" the librarian asked.

"In a way."

The librarian examined the book briefly, then slid it back across the desk to Patrick. "This book does not belong to Widener."

"I'm not returning it to Widener," Patrick said. "I'm returning it to Harry."

AUTHOR'S NOTE

This is a work of historical fiction. While it is based on actual events, I invented many of the main characters, including the Waters brothers, the Walsh family, Rockwell, and Berryman. But as I'm sure you know, *Titanic* was very real, so I spent countless hours researching the details of her construction, maiden voyage, and eventual demise to make the story of the great ship as accurate as possible. And the inspiration for this book came from an actual passenger and his peculiar life and death.

On the night *Titanic* sank, April 15, 1912, more than 1,500 people died, including a wealthy book collector named Harry Elkins Widener. I have been fascinated by Harry's story since I first heard about him when I was a student at Harvard University. Harry was only twenty-seven years old when he died, but he had already built a collection of more than 3,000 books. These weren't simply books, though. They were rare books.

When any book is first printed—including this one—only a certain number of copies are produced. Those originals, or first printings, are often lost or damaged, and people like Harry pay tremendous sums to preserve them in their private collections. You could go to a bookstore today and buy a copy of Robert Louis Stevenson's *Treasure Island* for $10. But Harry's first edition of *Treasure Island* would sell for at least $30,000!

After *Titanic* sank, Harry's mother donated a small fortune to Harvard so that the school would build a library in his honor. That building, the Harry Elkins Widener Memorial Library, still serves as Harvard's main library, and its intellectual centerpiece, nearly one hundred years later. It is home to more than 3 million books, including Harry's personal collection of works by Shakespeare, Charles Dickens, and his favorite, Robert Louis Stevenson. One book, however, is missing.

Shortly before Harry boarded *Titanic*, he visited a famous London book dealer named Bernard Quaritch. Harry had arranged to pick up a number of books, one of which was a rare edition of Sir Francis Bacon's *Essaies*. This story is true; Quaritch recounted it after Harry's death.

I don't know if there was a secret message hidden within that book, but Sir Francis Bacon was a master of codes and Harry clearly prized the *Essaies*. Although he asked Quaritch to ship most of his new volumes back to his family's Philadelphia mansion, he slipped the *Essaies* into his pocket and declared that he would keep the book with him if he were ship-wrecked.

A portrait of Harry Widener from Harvard's 1907 Class Album, five years before his death.

After Harry's death, every-one assumed that Bacon's *Essaies* sank with *Titanic*. One legend contends that he had secured a seat in a lifeboat when he realized he'd forgot-ten the book, so he raced back to his cabin to retrieve it and was never seen again. The *Essaies* may have perished that night, but I'd like to believe they survived. In reading about Harry, I learned that the Widener Library did have a rare second edition of the very same book. Immediately I started wondering: What if this was really Harry's copy? How could the *Essaies* have survived that night?

Dangerous Waters is my attempt to answer those questions.

3/10/12.

Dear Mr. Livingston-

Just a few lines to tell you that I am about to
make a quick trip to England. We sail on Wednesday
at 1. a. m. on the Mauretania and return on April
10th. on the Maiden voyage of the Titanic. So you
see we will only have a little over two weeks on
shore, all of which I expect to spend in London.
I hope to see Shorter, Wise, Gosse, and several
other collectors while there as I enjoyed them
so much last summer that I hope to
repeat the experience.

As for buying any books I don't expect to do much,
as I am saving every cent I can for the next
Huth sale, where I am really hoping to get
a number of books. Still I shall no doubt
see all the dealers and if I see a real bargain
I shall probably be unable to resist. Did I tell
you that when Quaritch was here I bought
the complete set of original drawings for
"Edwin Drood." They are wonderful and I am
very anxious to have you see them. I also

hope that when I get home in April you will
be around again for I have certainly missed
you during my trips to New York.

Now I will tell you a secret only you must
tell no one until it is out – grandfather has
bought the floe copy on paper of the Mazarin
Bible. Is it not great?! I wish it was
for me but it is not.

There is no other news but I look forward to
seeing you on my return. Please give my
best regards to Mrs. Livingston.

Yours sincerely

Harry E. Widener

P.S. I am glad you liked the little R.L.S. I
am very well pleased with it. Mrs. Strong can
make no fuss as Colvin gave me it and I
printed it after legal advice.

In this letter to book dealer Luther Livingston, Harry explains that he
is about to make a "quick trip to England" and will return on "on the
maiden voyage of the *Titanic*." During his visit he met with London
dealer Bernard Quartich—mentioned here—and bought a number of
books, including Sir Francis Bacon's *Essaies*.

The "little R.L.S." Harry refers to in the postscript is Robert Louis
Stevenson's partially complete autobiography. Harry owned Stevenson's
manuscript and paid to have it printed on fine paper for his friends and
associates, including Livingston.

At the end of the letter, Harry also reveals that his grandfather has
recently purchased a copy of "the Mazarin Bible"; today we call these
Gutenberg Bibles and they are the most expensive books in the world.
Only 23 complete copies remain and each is worth more than $25
million. The copy his grandfather purchased now resides in Widener
Library and is on display in a special case in front of Harry's portrait.

TITANIC

Monday, April 1

Titanic's first sea trials are postponed due to rough weather.

Tuesday, April 2

The ship successfully sails out into the Irish Sea, then returns to the Belfast Lough. That night, having passed her tests, the ship leaves for Southampton, England.

Wednesday, April 3

Titanic arrives in Southampton shortly after midnight. For the next week, *Titanic* is stocked with supplies and readied for her maiden voyage.

Wednesday, April 10

After the first passengers board, *Titanic* departs at noon. She nearly collides with another ship, then steams out of Southampton and anchors off Cherbourg, France, to load more passengers, including Harry Elkins Widener and his parents.

Thursday, April 11

Titanic makes her final stop, off the coast of Queenstown, Ireland, to take on additional passengers. That afternoon, she heads for the open ocean.

TIMELINE

Sunday, April 14   Throughout the day, *Titanic* receives numerous warnings of ice in the area. At 11:40 that evening, the ship strikes an iceberg on her starboard side. She begins to flood.

Monday, April 15   The first lifeboat is lowered into the sea at 12:45 AM. The water continues to rise, and at approximately 2:20 AM, *Titanic* sinks.

Carpathia receives *Titanic*'s distress signals and races to the site, rescuing the first group of passengers shortly after 4:00 AM.

Thursday, April 18   *Carpathia* arrives in New York with *Titanic*'s survivors.

1915

Thursday, June 24   The Harry Elkins Widener Memorial Library opens at Harvard College.

Titanic was designed to impress. Only three of her tall funnels actually spouted smoke from the furnaces below. The fourth, on the far left, was purely for show.

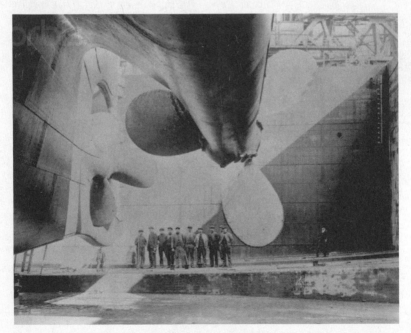

Here are two of the three great propellers that pushed *Titanic* through the sea. Inside the ship, trimmers like James Waters had to keep the furnaces burning to spin the blades.

The bright, colorful Reading Room, designed for women to relax and socialize, was the opposite of the men's dark, wooden smoking quarters. Patrick longs to be one of those men, so he is devastated when he's sent to work in the Reading Room. Yet that's where he first meets Emily and begins his friendship with Harry.

Harold Bride, the wireless operator Patrick gets to know, was a real member of *Titanic's* crew. Bride survived by climbing aboard a collapsible lifeboat, but one of his feet was terribly frostbitten from the icy water. Here he's pictured being helped up the ramp of the rescue ship, *Carpathia*.

ACKNOWLEDGMENTS

Thanks to Clare, Eleanor, and Dylan, for love, perspective, distractions and laughs; Mom and Dad, for unwavering support; Eighth Street Investments; the little Meridians; my junior editorial consultant; Coffee Exchange; Aldo's; Shem and Shaun; Nina and Pops; Orient and the Vineyard; Simtech; Valentina; Gillis; Chasson; westegg.com; Rachel Howarth and the helpful staff at Harvard's Houghton Library; Ken Wright, for bright ideas and feedback; Simon Boughton and Katherine Jacobs, for inspired editorial guidance. And thanks especially to Nika, for everything.